Anywhere, Everywhere

Renee MacKenzie

Anywhere, Everywhere

Renee MacKenzie

Affinity
eBook Press
NZ
2016

Anywhere, Everywhere

© Renee MacKenzie 2016

Affinity E-Book Press NZ LTD
Canterbury, New Zealand

1st Edition

ISBN: 978-0-908351-51-0

All rights reserved.

No part of this e-Book may be reproduced in any form without the express permission of the author and publisher. Please note that piracy of copyrighted materials violate the author's rights and is Illegal.

This is a work of fiction. Names, character, places, and incidents are the product of the author's imagination or are used fictitiously and any resemblance to actual persons living or dead, businesses, companies, events, or locales is entirely coincidental

Editor: Nat Burns
Proof Editor: Alexis Smith
Cover Design: Irish Dragon Designs

Acknowledgments

I would like to thank the Affinity eBooks Press team for their continued support and hard work on getting my books out there. Thank you Julie, Mel, and Nancy for being part of a brilliant publishing family. Thanks to Nat Burns for the superb editing, Irish Dragon Designs for another masterful cover, Alexis Smith for great proof editing, and Robin Hicks for her support over the last several books.

I would like to thank the following people for getting me out on the water and to the Ten Thousand Islands: Gary and Ellen Eichler of Double R's Manatee & Fishing Tours, Captain Jim Stiber of Everglades Charter Adventures, Ron and Christine Clark, and Kim and Mary of Island Girls Charters. Your love of the area shines through and you each shared something unique with me, and for that I will always be grateful.

Thanks Jack Shealy of Everglades Adventure Tours and Kit Carrington for talking to me about growing up in the Everglades. Thanks Kit also for being my early reader. Thanks Steve Fox for taking a look at this the first time I started it. Thank you Christine Clark for looking over my island facts. Thanks to John Kellam, Jim Burch, and Billy Snyder for helping me with some very important details. Thank you Captain Eddie for spending so much time talking to me about your cement houseboat; the information you provided was phenomenal.

And lastly, I'd like to thank the readers who have cheered me on along the way and shown me so much love. Thank you.

Dedication

For Pam. Always.

Table of Contents

Chapter One	1
Chapter Two	30
Chapter Three	51
Chapter Four	64
Chapter Five	75
Chapter Six	101
Chapter Seven	111
Chapter Eight	128
Chapter Nine	155
Chapter Ten	172
Chapter Eleven	193
Chapter Twelve	207
Chapter Thirteen	213
Chapter Fourteen	223
Chapter Fifteen	244
About the Author	248
Other Books from Affinity eBook Press	249

Also by Renee MacKenzie

23 Miles
Nesting
Confined Spaces
Flight

Anywhere, Everywhere

Chapter One

Gwen Martin paddled her kayak toward the marina, past the B-dock, approaching a lone brown pelican that was squatting on a piling. The wooden post was marred by streaks of gray and white bird droppings, proof of the pelican's frequent presence. The large bird's gaze followed her as she passed.

She rested the paddle across her kayak and watched as a slender figure walked down the A-dock. Without taking her eyes off the woman, Gwen yanked at the Velcro on her left glove, pulling it tighter, and then refastened it.

She smiled as the woman slowly advanced down the floating dock, pulling a large suitcase behind her. Gwen wondered if the size of the suitcase meant she was staying for an extended time or that she was just an over-packer. The woman paused in front of Eric Brown's thirty-nine foot Bayliner and looked from the sleek boat to the paper in her hand. Gwen knew exactly what she was thinking when she reluctantly renewed her journey down the wooden planks of the floating dock.

Gwen lingered, curious about why her heart was pounding at the very sight of this woman. *Get a grip*, she chastised herself. She let her gaze travel along the lean legs, the long, dark hair, the swell of breasts under the just-tight-enough T-shirt.

She floated on the gentle water, not wanting to leave behind the image of this attractive woman. And, she was more than a little curious to see the beautiful woman's response when she realized the boat she was looking for was the cement monstrosity at the very end of the dock. Gwen was pretty sure she was looking for *Ruffled Feathers* as no other boat could accommodate her massive suitcase.

The woman stared at the forty-one foot cement houseboat, and then glanced again at the paper in her hand. Her shoulders sagged when the key she pulled from her shorts' pocket unlocked the door without a problem. Instead of opening the door, she pulled out her cell phone.

Cell phone coverage around the marina was spotty at best, and there was no signal at the end of the A-dock. Gwen was aware of every gap in coverage at the marina. And she knew the big, cement houseboat better than anyone else. The woman's presence also explained why Walker had been airing out *Ruffled Feathers* a few days earlier.

She would have loved to keep watching the mystery woman, but she had to get to work. She pointed her kayak in the direction of the marina and paddled hard. After one last look behind her, seeing the woman staring at the boat with her hands on her hips, she drifted toward the boat ramp. She let her paddle drag just before she sent a gentle shower of water onto a black vulture.

"Shoo, sweetie," she said in a low voice. "I promise not to take your fish head."

The vulture hopped several feet to its left, still on the concrete ramp but out of Gwen's way. She was always amused by the hunched, bald-headed scavengers. "Come back later and gross out the tourists," she added.

Gwen climbed out of the kayak, careful not to slip on the scum-mottled ramp. She dragged her kayak the rest of the way up, then off to the side where it'd be out of the way of folks launching their boats. She slipped the paddle into the boat's hull, then pulled off her fingerless gloves and shoved them into the back pocket of her Columbia shorts. She took the bandana from around her neck and retied it on her head, assuring her chin-length, blondish hair would stay out of her face and be somewhat protected from the incidental yuck always present at the marina. As she walked toward the ship's store, she tucked her fishing shirt into her shorts.

She willed herself not to look back to the A-dock. Her resolve only lasted until she stepped between the live shrimp tank and the frozen bait freezer at the front door. She glanced to where she last saw the mystery woman and was disappointed when she didn't see her. Gwen couldn't help but wonder if the woman was inside the boat, appreciating the fine detail and workmanship of the interior, or was still disgusted by the not so fine details of the exterior of *Ruffled Feathers*. Her heart started pounding again and she realized she cared more than she could explain about what this woman thought of the remodeling work Gwen had done to the boat that had once belonged to her family.

Gwen checked the freezer door and gave it a push to close it the rest of the way. She hated that neither customers nor Herb, her boss, would take the moment needed to ensure that the freezer was completely closed. She pulled open the door to the ship's store and steeled herself before walking in.

I will not tell Herb to kiss my butt. I will not threaten to throw any tourists or fishermen off the seawall. I will not quit this job that I unfortunately need more than I care to admit, she thought, as she did each workday.

She rounded the fishing pole display and right away saw Herb kicked back in the chair behind the counter, his arms resting on his protruding belly, chin almost touching his chest, obviously napping. It was March, and things were starting to slow down, but it wasn't off-season enough for him to already be pulling his sleeping beauty act.

"Shrimp been culled?" she asked, louder than necessary.

Herb's head jerked up. "What?"

She stared at the brown snuff juice stain discoloring the deep line leading from the corner of his mouth and disappearing into his sagging chin. She cringed. "I asked if the shrimp's been culled."

"Nah, ain't had time."

Gwen logged into the register and clicked on the total sales for the morning. *$113.15 and he 'ain't had time?'*

She grabbed a plastic grocery bag from the rack beside the register before heading for the door. "I'll be culling," she called out as she left.

She opened the lid to the shrimp tank and propped it up with a thin, metal rod. A quick assessment told her that the breeze wouldn't be an issue. She hated windy days when the rod holding up the lid would often shift and the flimsy top would come down on her head.

Gwen stuck the plastic grocery bag into the small bucket, using the bag as a liner. Movement to her right caught her attention and she turned as an iridescent boat-tailed grackle perched on the side of the tank. "Don't even think about it, buddy," she said to the bird. The grackles were smart, and could get pretty bold. She'd seen them climb down the aeration tubing to the surface of the water in the tank and snatch shrimp right up. She'd also seen them perch on the side of a distracted fisherman's bait bucket and help themselves.

"Shoo," she said.

It flew a few feet away and continued to keep watch.

She grabbed the net from the hook on the side of the tank and started scooping. As she picked out the dead shrimp, she counted them before throwing them into the bag. Gently releasing the live shrimp back into the tank, she scooped again, repeating the process.

"Hey, sweetheart, I'll take five dozen of your largest shrimp." The man set his bait bucket at Gwen's feet as he leaned against the shrimp tank.

Gwen kept a silent count in her head as she pulled another dead shrimp from the net and tossed it into the bag. She glanced up and smiled at her uncle, Derek Hanes. When he lingered without showing any sign of recognition, she spoke. "Good morning, Mr. Hanes. You can pay inside, then bring the receipt out with you."

"What'cha doing with those dead ones?" he asked.

Ninety-one, ninety-two, ninety-three, she counted to herself.

"Oh, sorry, hope I didn't make you lose count. Hey, didn't the state buy this place?" he barked out.

Ninety-five, ninety-six. She smiled at him, preparing to answer the question he'd asked her every day since he'd buried his wife seven months earlier. "No, sir," she said. "The county was going to buy the marina but the deal fell through."

"How do you feel about working for the state?"

It's the county, not the state, and it isn't happening.

"I'm sure it'll all be just fine. How about I get your five dozen shrimp for you while you go inside and pay?"

"Make 'em big ones," he told her as he pulled open the front door.

Gwen reached across the tank and knocked on the window with the end of the shrimp net. When Herb looked up she held up five fingers. She sighed. Her uncle Derek had really deteriorated during the past couple of years. Even though it wasn't uncommon for people to be confused about who the marina belonged to after a few unrealized deals, usually she only had to correct them once. And it wasn't just the same questions he repeatedly asked. The man's personality had altered negatively as well. And then there was him not knowing who she was most of the time, despite the fact that she had lived with him and her Aunt Linda from the time she was seven until she turned eighteen and left for college.

She grabbed his bait bucket and dipped it in the tank to get some of the salty water, then she counted out five dozen shrimp, and added a few more lively ones for good measure.

She pushed the bucket of bait off to the side and resumed her silent count of dead shrimp.

"Twenty, forty, eleven," a man's voice teased her from behind.

"Screw you, Wyatt." She didn't even bother to look at her brother.

Wyatt laughed. "You about done?"

She threw one more into the bag. "One hundred and thirty three." She tied the top of the bag and handed it to him.

"Thanks, little sister."

"Just promise you'll behave yourself."

He gave her his trademark smile, the half-smile that was charming on him, but awkward on her. She'd tried most of her life to train herself to smile differently. Sometimes she managed, most times she didn't.

"It ain't about behaving, it's about not getting caught," Wyatt said.

"Yeah, and that attitude's really gotten you far."

"About as far as yours has, little sister," he teased.

She dismissed him with a flick of her hand. "Now go. Take your smelly chumming shrimp and get out of my way. I've got filters to clean."

"Yes, ma'am," he said with a slight bow.

"Oh, and Wyatt, could you keep an eye on Uncle Derek out there today?"

"He don't even know who I am half the time. Besides, I ain't nobody's keeper."

"Please?" she added.

He just scowled at her, but she knew he'd do it. She watched him retreat, thinking his hair, two or three inches longer than her own, was getting too shaggy. His stomach was showing a few too many beers. She hoped drinking was the only one of his vices in which he was indulging. At least now that Tracy was long gone from his life he was staying out of trouble for the most part. It saddened her that they had watched Wyatt's girlfriend spin out of control with drug addiction, and how she'd almost dragged Wyatt down with her.

Gwen reached into the back corner of the tank and pulled off the filter. Then she grabbed the one in the other corner and carried them both to the fish cleaning station. Moments after she turned on the hose, an immature brown pelican landed in the water in front of her. As she watched him swim back and forth, begging for a handout, his anxiety washed over her, manifesting itself in a slight prickling in her arms. She wondered what that was about. She hadn't even touched him.

"Come on, you goof. Bobbing around down there just makes you gator bait." Gwen kept her voice gentle, but on the inside she raged against the idiots who fed the pelicans, making the big, awkward birds vulnerable by getting them to hang around in the brackish water where the gators prowled. She should show tough love to the pelican, but couldn't bring herself to spray it with the hose or do anything else to drive it away.

She kept one eye on the bird as she rinsed out the strips of blue filter material littered with mushy shrimp waste. As she reassembled the filters, she watched the pelican fly to the nearest dock. The chunky bird waddled around the B-dock until it found just the right spot to settle.

She saw her uncle walking toward the boat that he probably shouldn't have been driving.

"You're a good girl," he called to her. "I hope the state gives you a big raise."

"Thank you," she answered, not bothering to correct him. "Good luck out there."

Gwen made her way back into the store after reattaching the shrimp filters, thankful when she saw that Herb was nowhere around. She pulled up the shrimp inventory spreadsheet on the desktop and entered her count from earlier. She noticed Herb had added a large number to the dead column the day before. There was a note in the column next to it that they had had a massive die-off, maybe due to the water in the tanks getting too hot. That just meant Herb was trying to hide the fact that he charged people for their shrimp and pocketed the money instead of ringing it up. She just shrugged it off. The last person who had told the owner about the skimming had been fired by Herb in less than a week. If the owner was going to tell Herb everything the employees told him, Gwen would just continue to let Herb steal from him. It wasn't her problem.

She turned around when she heard a clank on the glass countertop by the register. "Hello," Gwen said to a man she thought she recognized. Some folks she knew by name, some by face, and some not at all, but she tried to make everyone feel welcomed. She scanned the barcode on the six-pack of Corona and took his money.

"Have a great day," she said.

He held up the beer. "I will now," he said with a scowl.

Gwen hung around the register until Herb reappeared, then went out to sweep the sidewalks. She'd just finished the front walk and rounded the corner to the side facing the docks when she saw her. The mystery woman was walking slowly down the wood planks, staring at her cell phone as she went.

"No signal yet, babe," Gwen whispered as she leaned against the broom, watching as the woman paused again in front of Eric's slick boat. She slowly continued to sweep while keeping her eyes firmly fixed on the woman's long legs. "Go toward the mangroves," she quietly coached her.

The woman stepped off the dock and turned to the right.

"There you go. A few more steps."

The woman took three more steps and stopped near the mangroves. She dialed. Gwen watched as she spoke into her cell. Her free hand gestured in a manner that told Gwen the woman was not happy.

A breeze blew through and the woman ran her hand over her blowing hair. Gwen wondered how that hair would feel between her fingers. She unconsciously adjusted the bandana on her own head as she briefly entertained the idea of bringing the woman a ball cap from the ship's store as a welcome-to-the-marina present. Thinking the woman might have just packed heavily and would only be there a few days, she quickly dismissed the idea.

"Hey, honey," Herb's deep voice boomed.

Gwen bristled at the greeting. "Hey," she answered.

"When you get done out here, someone tracked mud all through the store." He took several steps in her direction as he spoke. She took a few steps backward, keeping the broom in position between them in a silent quest for space.

"I really like that color on you," he said as he motioned to her bandana. "It brings out the green of your eyes." His gaze traveled much lower than her eyes.

She decided to burn the bandana when she got home.

"But those shorts." He smiled, revealing tobacco-specked, stained teeth. "They'd be nicer if they were a little shorter."

She cringed. *Go away, go away, go away*, she chanted in her mind.

"I'm leaving. Don't forget the beer guy will be here tomorrow. Get the cooler cleaned up before then."

She concentrated on sweeping around what appeared to be snuff spit on the sidewalk. "Yeah, sure," she muttered.

She swept for several more minutes before Peter, a regular customer, handed Gwen his bait bucket. "The last batch all died. That happens a lot. Do I get these ones for free?"

"You'd have to talk to Herb. He's already left for the day." She took the bucket to the shrimp tank and dipped it in for some of the saltwater.

"No water. Just shrimp," Peter said.

"Have you been putting the shrimp in your live well?"

"Yeah," he muttered.

"Using that water?" she asked.

"Ah, yeah – duh," he said.

"That water isn't salty enough to keep the shrimp alive until you get out to the gulf. The problem hasn't been the shrimp, but the water. That's why we always try to give you some of our water with the shrimp." She kept the water in the bucket. "How many?"

"Three dozen." He crossed his arms in a move that always made Gwen think of grown men pouting like children. "Thanks," he muttered almost under his breath.

†

"My God, Jeremy, what were you thinking? I'm in the middle of nowhere and the boat you rented is hideous." Piper Jackson turned toward the houseboat and cringed. At first glance, the boat appeared to be made of plaster, but the closer she looked, she saw that it was cement. While all the boats around it were slick and shiny, this one was dull and faded. It was mostly a whitish color, but with faded red or brown on the lower fourth and the trim.

"Hey, I'm trying to take care of this," Jeremy said. "Now, quit your bitching. It was *you* who wouldn't back down on that story. It's *you* they want dead now. I'm just trying to keep you alive. I told you to leave Bronson alone, Piper."

"Yeah, after you put me on his trail. You're the one who told me something hinky was going on with Bronson. And you know how I get when my curiosity is piqued. I'm like a dog with a bone." She held the cell phone with one hand and fended off a fly with the other. "And it's not Piper, remember? Hell, you're the one who came up with PJ," she said.

"Well, just lay low down there. Please, *PJ*?"

"Lay low?" she growled. "How can someone lay low on the most conspicuous boat in the marina?" She swatted at a fly. Pesky, but nothing compared to the mosquitoes the past summer in Virginia.

"I didn't know anything about the boat. The friend of a friend of a friend rented it to me at a really good price. And it was as far away as I could get you without you having to learn a foreign language."

"Don't be so sure of yourself. I got lost in Miami on my way down here and couldn't find anyone in any of the drug stores, fast food joints, or gas stations who spoke English." She swatted at the yellow fly that kept going for her eyes.

"But you got there safely and that's what counts. You left the car in the parking lot in Naples and took a cab to the marina, right?"

"Yeah."

"Is the boat that bad?" Jeremy asked.

She looked at the atrocious cement houseboat. "Yes." When she thought of the built-in bookshelves, the ornate headboard, the fact that the inside had obviously been redone recently, she softened. "Okay, maybe it's not *that* bad."

"Just make the most of it for now. Please?"

She sighed. As her best friend and ex-husband, Jeremy just wanted what was best for her and she knew that. "I'll be fine here. At least it has a microwave."

"See, there's a plus. And please be careful. I mean it."

"Yep. Careful." She took a deep breath and let her gaze travel across the marina to where the woman she'd seen earlier wielded a broom. She had also watched the woman when she'd held the broom between her and a large man, almost as if she was protecting herself with it. Piper had studied them. It didn't take a genius to figure out that the big guy was a bullying creep, and the hot woman was working hard to keep her distance without insulting the man who probably signed her paycheck.

A breeze caught Piper's hair. It felt wonderful, but after only a few moments it turned into wind. She decided to quit bitching at him and go inside her cement abode. "Okay, Jeremy. I'll call you tomorrow." She looked around her at the unusual mix of retirees and salty fishing types, the juxtaposition of old boats like her temporary home and the expensive, brand spanking new ones. "This is a strange little place."

"Just don't become complacent. Bronson's goons are dangerous people. As you well know."

A shudder passed through Piper. Yes, she had seen just how dangerous they were. "I'll be vigilant. I promise."

"You're my favorite ex-wife and I love you."

"I'm your only ex-wife. Unless something has happened between you and Anthony?"

"No, we're great."

"Good. And I love you, too."

She glanced one last time at the marina employee as she disconnected. She made her way down the dock to the houseboat, noting the building clouds in the direction where she imagined rested the Gulf of Mexico. She grabbed the aluminum railing as she stepped up onto the walkway that went most of the way around the boat.

Inside, Piper powered up her laptop. Maybe she'd play some solitaire to pass the time. She really wanted to find some Wi-Fi and get online. Her curiosity about this part of southwest Florida was getting the better of her. She'd go crazy if she didn't at least look into the area.

She missed Jeremy. They hadn't been apart more than a week at a time since the sixth grade. When Piper's family moved in next door to Jeremy's, the two became instant best friends, and inseparable in their small town in Virginia. They went to prom together, and fell into bed afterward. That summer, when Piper learned she was pregnant, Jeremy proposed. His proposal was awkward and cryptic. He told Piper he loved her and wanted to raise their baby together, but added that she had to know up front that he was who he was and wouldn't change. She'd had no idea what he'd meant. So, they married, him assuming she'd always known he was gay, and her assuming that their marriage would be fine even though they hadn't had sex since their drunken romp on prom night.

Piper lost the baby two months after they'd married. She'd gone on to get her education at the local community college, and he'd moved up in the ranks at the local furniture store. Life was comfortable. Then she caught Jeremy in bed with a man. She was hurt and confused, but they got through it. She'd had to admit to herself that, in her heart, she'd known he was gay, she just didn't want to give him up. Or face the truth about herself.

They'd stayed comfortably married. Their marriage fooled his bigoted family, and helped her business. It seemed to Piper that the people in their town who could afford the services of a professional photographer loved the idea of having a gay man arrange the flowers, but didn't want a dyke pointing her lens at the young, innocent brides. But then Jeremy met Anthony and Piper just felt in the way. So, they'd divorced. He had stayed with Anthony. She had plenty of women in her life. And Piper and Jeremy remained best friends.

A clap of thunder rattled the windows of the houseboat. She let out a nervous chuckle at how she'd jumped at the crashing noise. "Don't get spooked," she told herself. "Vigilance is not the same as paranoia," she chastised. "Damned Bronson."

Piper took several deep breaths in an attempt to calm herself. Instead, her mind rammed back to the night her life had changed so drastically.

She'd been sitting in her Dodge Dakota half a block from where Bronson's meeting with an informant was going down. She'd already taken good identifying photos of the informant, Bronson, and two of the latter man's goons. It was the beginning of March and quite cold in the car. She didn't dare leave it running with the heat on, not wanting to give away her location. She'd smelled pizza and wished that whatever was going to happen would just hurry up and happen so she could get a hot, cheesy medium pizza with black olives and mushrooms.

When the muscle-bound goon slammed the balding informant against the rough, brick wall, Piper's hunger went into check and her instincts kicked in. She took shot after shot of the muscled guy and his skinny cohort punching the informant. Then, in perfect telephoto focus, Bronson shot the man between the eyes.

Piper zoomed in close on the man and took a shot of his face. She knew the second she took the photo that he was dead. She sent anonymous copies to the police three days before the local paper published the story with her byline. She was naïve enough to think that Joseph Bronson would be behind bars before the story ran. But Joseph Bronson went underground. And Piper was running for her life.

The roar of rain brought her out of her reverie.

Anywhere, Everywhere

"What have I done?" she asked herself. Her first attempt at photojournalism and it had to be a murder? She was way out of her league. She should have stuck to photographing snobby weddings, even if the bridezillas drove her crazy. She'd just been so intrigued when her camera captured the perfect, tell-all, smoldering look between the groom and one of the bridesmaids. She couldn't keep herself from including the shot with the others she sent to the bride for proofing. She'd known from the moment she saw the image of the inappropriate exchange between the groom and bridesmaid that simple wedding photography would never again be enough. Surely, freelance photojournalism would be the answer to all her problems.

Then it became her biggest problem. Bronson was out there somewhere, and he wanted her dead. She shivered. What if the cops couldn't find Bronson before he found her? Another noise startled her. She took a deep breath before pushing the curtain aside and peering out of the galley window. The woman at the marina was securing the trashcans outside of the store. Sheets of rain assailed the blonde, plastering her bright green bandana to her head.

Piper couldn't help but appreciate how the woman's drenched fishing shirt clung to her, showing the outline of a tank top and well-toned arms. Maybe she'd found just the distraction she needed to keep her mind off her problems. Ah, she could hope…

†

Gwen wiped the rain from her eyes and squinted in the direction of *Ruffled Feathers*. She saw the curtain part and felt the mystery woman watching her. She hated that Herb had interrupted her study of the woman earlier.

She stole another glance toward *Ruffled Feathers* and wondered what the mystery woman was doing inside. She felt the familiar bitterness rise in her as she reformed the thought into wondering what the woman was doing inside *her* boat. Their father had put *Ruffled Feathers* in Wyatt's name right before he was busted. Wyatt was only seventeen at the time. Just a kid. And he didn't take care of the houseboat. Then, two years ago, Wyatt offered half the boat to Gwen. He told her if she remodeled the inside, when she was done he'd make her co-owner and let her live on it. She'd worked hard for more than a year to get it fixed up. She'd had to work slowly since she didn't have a lot of money to invest. So, as she got the cash, she'd put it and a bunch of elbow grease into the interior of *Ruffled Feathers*. When she finished, she found out that Wyatt had lost the boat to Arnie Walker in a poker game. Her investment of time and money was for nothing.

By the time she flipped the closed sign on the front door of the store, the rain had stopped, as had the lightning. She didn't mind paddling in the rain, but knew better than to be on the water in a thunderstorm. She gave the floor a quick sweep after reconciling the cash register, then cleaned the bathrooms. After a final, visual once-over, she locked the store behind her.

She took a deep breath as she pulled on her paddling gloves. She loved the smell after a good rain, as well as the mist off the brackish water and the way the sun glinted off all the wet surfaces. After a last glance in the direction of the houseboat, she pushed the kayak to the edge of the water. As much as she got irritated with tourists and fishing guides, and as much as she disliked being around the lecherous Herb, she knew that not everyone had the good fortune to live in such a gorgeous place and to be able to kayak to work. She smiled as she climbed into her kayak and pushed off from the boat ramp.

She drifted past the three docks that stretched out like fingers and turned her kayak to face down the canal. Balancing her paddle across the top, she removed her bandana and pulled the fishing shirt over her head, leaving on her snug tank top. After she stuffed her clothing between the seat-back and life preserver, she combed her fingers through her hair and ruffled it. She squared her shoulders and grabbed her paddle.

She paddled hard until her arms burned and shoulders ached, then she paddled harder. This was her favorite part of the day. Nothing was more cleansing than working out hard and sweating out all the psychic toxins that had accumulated throughout the day. The burn in her arms intensified and she bore down with her legs against the inside of her boat. The sun on her face and the water running off her paddle into her lap brought a smile to her face. She lived for this feeling of strength and freedom.

As she neared home, she let up on the paddling and let her body start to cool down. She raised her arms above her head and smiled when the paddle dripped the brackish water down on her. After stretching out her arm muscles, she lowered the paddle back into the water, then dug deep with the left end of the paddle to turn the kayak toward the small break in the mangroves where she always beached. Just as she was about to make the push onto the dirt, she saw him.

Justice. Fourteen feet of cantankerous fierceness, Justice could lay his alligator self anywhere he chose to and get away with it. On this day, it seemed, he wanted to lie just enough in her path to make her uneasy about landing there.

"Come on, isn't there somewhere else you can sunbathe?" She sighed. Apparently not.

She backed the kayak up several feet – the farther from the mangroves, the fewer the bugs – and waited. Since it was getting late, she hoped Justice would be moving on soon. The growling of her stomach drove home just how much she hoped he'd tire of sunning there sooner rather than later.

A Carolina skiff made its way in her direction, going faster than it should. She would never get what part of no wake these people didn't understand. She recognized the driver as one of the regulars from the ship's store. He always bought the newspaper, a coffee, and two dozen shrimp when he came in.

When he waved, she resisted the temptation to yell at him. Instead, she nodded as she tried to keep her kayak facing into the wake. *Choose your battles*, Wyatt always told her. For once, she would listen to him. She gritted her teeth until the boat was gone and the water had settled.

Gwen was growing tired of the waiting game. She looked from a different angle to see if maybe she had more room between Justice and the mangroves than she thought. Not so much. Another belly rumble and she decided maybe she was wrong. She took in the position of his body, the set of his head, staring until he blurred in her vision and she felt his indifference. He wasn't interested in her as a meal, but didn't want to feel challenged by her either. She steeled her nerves and took a deep breath. She paddled with short, choppy strokes, keeping as far to the right of the path as she could as she beached onto the sand and shell path. Exiting on the right, she kept the kayak between her and Justice and dragged it up the bank.

Justice never budged. It was unnerving how still an alligator could remain. She cringed as she remembered a close call she'd witnessed the year before. A group of tourists had stopped their car half-on-half-off the road—ugh, one of her biggest pet peeves—and were taking pictures of what they must have believed to be a road-kill alligator. When they positioned Grandma close by for a photo and the creature moved, much screaming and scrambling for the car ensued.

Gwen carried the kayak farther up than usual, so as to keep it handy as a shield. When she was a safe distance from Justice, she dropped the kayak and whispered thanks to him. He made a growly-groany sound.

"You need to learn to share," she told the large reptile.

He let out a low, deep growl again, and launched himself off the bank and into the water.

She turned and jumped at the unexpected sight of her brother.

"Hey, little sister," Wyatt sang out from beside his truck.

"What are you doing here?" she asked.

"Is that any way to treat someone who comes bearing gifts?" He pretended to pout. "Here, take some of this fish."

She eyed the red snapper. It was at least twenty inches long, so at least he was legal in that sense. "No, thanks."

"Come on, I was respectful when I caught it." He flashed a smile.

She studied his face and the twitch below his left eye gave him away. "Liar."

He laughed. "Your loss. Take it or it'll be wasted. I don't think Mother Earth would like it to just get thrown away." He shoved it toward her.

"Stop it. I said I don't want it." She was about to slap his hand away when an alligator bellow got their attention. The deep, guttural noise was followed by a splashing ruckus. Gwen couldn't help herself. "Fucking or fighting?" she asked in their customary way.

"Fighting," Wyatt answered without missing a beat. "Definitely fighting." And with that, one of the large gators made a bee-line away from its adversary. "I guess you've noticed the hot chick renting *Ruffled Feathers*?"

Gwen acted like she didn't hear the question.

"Oh, don't even try to tell me you ain't noticed her."

Gwen shrugged as she looked directly at her brother. His half-smile egged her on. Finally, curiosity got the better of her. "So, what's her story?"

"I don't know. Nobody seems to know anything other than she's hot," Wyatt said.

Gwen walked toward the front door of her small home.

Her brother called after her. "I got first dibs!"

She waved him off without looking back. She tried to convince herself that the sudden pounding of her heart had nothing to do with the mention of the mystery woman. Gwen glanced at the shed that served as her woodworking shop. Ever since losing some of her tools, then *Ruffled Feathers*, she hadn't been in the mood to coax birds or animals out of the wood.

Once inside her small house, she opened the refrigerator and for just a moment wished she'd taken the fish. She pulled out two eggs. An omelet with free-range eggs and organic veggies would be perfect. Who cares if she'd had that for dinner just the day before?

†

Piper ran her fingertips across the nautical rope serving as trim on the kitchen cabinets. She liked those little details. And the ornate wood paneling on all the walls was gorgeous. She glanced at the couch. She'd been sleeping there instead of the queen-sized bed in the bedroom. With it being just her, she couldn't make herself sleep in the bedroom. The bedroom was smaller, about eight feet by eleven, and made her feel trapped. Sure, the couch was right by the door, which could make her vulnerable, but it still felt safer than the bedroom. But if she had the company of the marina woman it'd be a very different story. She'd gladly partake of the bed if she had the hot blonde there with her.

Piper sighed. If the marina woman was half as hot up-close as she was from a distance, then…yum. She'd seen the woman fiercely paddling her yellow kayak just an hour earlier. After stripping off her over-shirt and bandana, the woman had stretched tanned, muscular arms. The edges of a tattoo peeked out from under the tank top, adorning shoulders that looked powerful. Piper wanted to run her fingers over those muscles. A twinge of desire shot down her abdomen to settle between her legs.

She stood and paced the best she could in the cramped quarters. "I can't believe I'm hiding in here. I'm a hack," she said in a low voice. "I am a hack in *way* over my head." She stopped. Did she just hear something? No, of course not. "And now I'm a paranoid hack."

"Hello, aboard *Ruffled Feathers*," a man's voice called out.

She jumped. She double-checked that the door was locked before peeking around the edge of the curtains covering the round, porthole window.

"Hello," the man said, looking at her through the small opening in the cloth. "Welcome to the neighborhood."

The man wore nothing but cargo shorts and flip-flops. With one hand he stroked a tuft of hair beneath his lower lip, the other grasped a can of beer.

Her first thought was that he wasn't one of Bronson's goons because he couldn't possibly be concealing a weapon. Her second thought was that she hoped he wouldn't create a scene or draw any attention to her.

She pulled the curtain open a few inches and looked around, trying to ascertain if the man was alone.

"I was wondering if we could talk. My name is Wyatt. We're neighbors, sort of."

"I'd kind of just like to be left alone," Piper said.

"Give me a few minutes of your time and then I'll go away. I promise."

She fidgeted with the cell phone in the front pocket of her shorts. It wouldn't do her any good since she couldn't get a signal on the boat or the dock anyway.

"Come on out." He gestured around. "There are people around to make sure I don't do anything out of line."

She walked to the front of the boat, where the controls were, and reached to move aside the curtain there. Several men were gathered around the fish cleaning station. Judging by their hand movements, they were all telling their own versions of the fish that got away.

Might as well talk to him so he'll go away, she thought.

She unlocked the door and started to open it. It caught and wouldn't slide. She was getting tired of its resistance every time she tried to leave the boat.

"Here," the man said. He grabbed the edge of the wood door and lifted it. "This door is a little touchy, is all. Pull up on it as you begin to slide it open."

Piper stepped back when the door slid open toward the back of the boat. The man stood there smiling at her. He stepped back a few steps, making room for her to step down off the boat onto the dock. When he reached out his hand as if to help her, she grabbed the railing instead, then stepped onto the dock.

"Like I said, my name's Wyatt and we're sort of neighbors." He shifted his can of beer to his left hand and reached out his right one.

Piper hesitated before taking his hand to shake. "Hi."

He held on to her hand. "This is where you introduce yourself."

She pulled her hand away from his. "I'm PJ. And like I said, I'd rather just be left alone."

"Vacationing?"

She gripped the door frame. "Yeah, vacationing."

"If you step on out of the boat you could shut the door and keep from air-conditioning the entire Ten Thousand Island area. Or you could invite me in," he said with a smile.

He laughed when she quickly stepped onto the floating dock and slid the door shut behind her. "So, are you out here alone?"

She hesitated.

"I'm not asking so I can come back after dark and do terrible things to you. Unless you want me to." He laughed. "I'm asking 'cause I was wondering if you had any protection."

"Protection?"

"Like a gun. Do you have a gun?"

"I—do I—?"

"Do you want one?"

"Should I?" she asked.

"I know I wouldn't want my girlfriend out here at night without one." He gestured toward a truck. "Let me show you what I would recommend you have out here if you were my girlfriend or sister or whatever."

Piper watched as he ambled down the dock. It crossed her mind to just go back on the boat and lock the door behind her, but she had to admit she was curious about this guy. And he did seem harmless enough.

Wyatt grabbed a towel-covered bundle from the cab of a beat-up, old pick-up truck. He finished off his beer and threw the can in the bed of the truck before starting back down the dock.

"It sure would be better if we did this inside," Wyatt said.

Piper glanced at the boat, then at the men at the cleaning station. No one was paying them any attention. "Here's fine," she said.

He laughed. "Suit yourself." He squatted and placed the bundle on the dock. He unwrapped a revolver and a shotgun.

Her heart started to pound. He picked up the revolver. "If you're gonna wander around at night, I'd say go with this .38."

She saw an image of Bronson shooting the informant in the face and felt her breath catch in her chest.

"But if you'll be mostly staying put on the boat at night, the shotgun is a good choice." He stroked the length of it. "And I can give you a really good deal on this one."

As Wyatt showed her how to operate the shotgun, she kept sneaking peeks at him. His wavy, sun-bleached hair hung almost to his shoulders. Just below a crooked smile was a soul patch, that little area of hair below a man's lower lip that she always found herself watching if she spoke to someone with one. Soul patches distracted her as much as facial piercings did.

"If you don't pay attention, you ain't gonna know how to use it when you need it," Wyatt said.

The heat rose on Piper's face. God, she hoped her studying him didn't give him the wrong idea.

"You married?" Wyatt asked.

"No."

"Boyfriend?"

"No."

"Girlfriend?" As he asked the question, his attention turned to an old man struggling to pull a boat alongside the seawall by the marina.

"Not at this very moment." It flashed through her mind that the old man was at the spot where the marina woman had been cleaning something and talking to a pelican earlier.

Wyatt continued watching the old man. Piper was surprised by the ease at which he asked about a girlfriend, and equally surprised by how he didn't react to her answer. She shrugged it off, not even knowing if he'd heard her.

"So, what do you think?" Wyatt asked.

"About the gun?"

"Yeah," he smiled. "About the gun."

"I don't know." She looked around.

"It's amazing how much a person can relax when they know they can protect themselves," Wyatt said. "Seventy-five bucks is a real bargain. I'll even throw in a box of shells. And a free tutorial if you ever want a lesson on shooting it."

She glanced toward the door to the houseboat.

"Tell you what," Wyatt said. "You take it now, and I'll come back tomorrow for the money." He smiled. "You know, after you've had a chance to go to the ATM."

"Okay," Piper answered. "Come back tomorrow and I'll pay you then." She had the cash hidden under the couch cushion on the boat but wasn't about to let this guy know that.

"And can I be of any further service to you?"

"Can you tell me where to get decent coffee around here?"

"Define decent. The ship's store has fresh, no frills coffee all day."

"I guess there isn't a sushi bar with Wi-Fi anywhere around here?"

Wyatt gestured past the store. "The hotel right through there has a restaurant and bar. And Wi-Fi. Problem is the restaurant is iffy, the bar is expensive, and the Wi-Fi is for guests and needs a code."

"Good to know," Piper said.

"Go into Naples or Marco for the sushi. A couple of the restaurants in Everglades might have Wi-Fi."

"Everglades? As in the swamp?"

"No, as in Everglades City. Just east of here. But beware the drug smugglers."

"What?"

He laughed. "A joke. I was poking fun at the outside world's stereotypes of people from Everglades City. Humor?"

Silence.

"Never mind," he said.

Chapter Two

Gwen placed the folded and bagged fishing shirt on the bottom of the kayak, between her feet. She figured there was no sense in getting all of her clothes dirty before she even made it to work. She stashed the towel needed to calm the bird beside her shirt. A boater who lived near the marina had called earlier to let her know that a pelican had been hooked and was struggling to fly near one of the docks. He believed the fishing line was wrapped around at least one wing, and originated from a hook embedded in its bill. One more reason why it was so wrong to feed the pelicans – when they associated people with food, they couldn't differentiate between a handout and someone's catch.

As she approached the marina, she saw the floundering bird ahead. She paddled along the A-dock, being careful to go in gently. She didn't want to ram the dock or alarm the pelican.

"Hey, sweetie, look at you all tangled up," she whispered.

She felt the beginning of the wake at the same time she heard the engine. She waved her paddle in the boat's direction, but the boat just roared by. The pelican tried to take flight from its position on the water, but instead was pitched against the dock. Gwen reached for the bird, but the motion, combined with the waves from the passing boat, caused the kayak to flip. She slipped her legs free and pushed the boat away in an attempt to keep it from hitting her.

In one fluid, reactive movement, she propelled herself onto the dock. Being raised in southwest Florida, she knew better than to be complacent on the water. She took a deep breath and walked to the slip where the pelican struggled. She sprawled on her belly across the wood planks and reached into the water to stabilize the large, awkward bird. It had just registered in her mind that she was at *Ruffled Feather's* slip when she heard the sound of a gun cocking.

"Don't fucking move," a woman's voice demanded.

Gwen didn't like the quiver of fear she heard in the voice behind her. Experience taught her that a scared person with a gun was more dangerous than a confident one. "Um – if I don't move, that ten-foot gator swimming this way is going to eat this bird *and* my arm," Gwen said. In her peripheral vision, she saw the woman take a step back. Gwen took advantage of her distraction and jumped up. Within seconds she had the gun in her right hand, and her left arm around the woman's waist. "Whoa, easy," she whispered, as they faltered near the edge of the dock.

"What were you doing to my boat?"

"*Your* boat?" Gwen asked.

"I'm renting it." She stiffened. "What were you doing?"

"Trying to save a pelican. Now if you don't mind, I'd like to get back to it." She turned to the water and sighed at the sight of her capsized kayak.

The woman reached for the gun and Gwen held it just out of her reach. Gwen's attention went to the heat growing between their bodies. They were the same height, and fit perfectly together. She saw a flicker of something cross the woman's face and wondered if maybe the same thought....

"Are you two fucking or fighting?" Wyatt called out as he walked down the dock.

Gwen pressed the length of the shotgun into the woman and marveled at the blush that ran up the woman's neck. "Here. And for God's sake, be careful with the thing," she said to her. She looked at Wyatt. "Help or go away."

"Help with what?" he asked as he craned his neck.

"Hooked pelican."

"I ain't aiding and abetting a flying rat." He crinkled his nose as he spoke.

"You're the only rat. Now go away if you aren't going to help."

She turned her back on her brother and spoke to the woman. "Do you have an old towel I can borrow? I need to place a towel on its head to help calm it and keep it from hurting itself or me." Her eyes drifted from the woman's mouth to the gun. "Could you put that thing away and give me a hand?" she asked, her voice low.

The woman nodded and bolted onto the boat. She came back out with a large, plush towel. "It's the only kind I have," she said, when Gwen stared at it.

Gwen smiled. "It'll do just fine."

"I don't know anything about these things."

Gwen warmed at the woman's obvious nervousness. "I'll guide you," she said with a reassuring smile. "My name's Gwen."

"I'm PJ."

The hooked pelican's erratic movements returned Gwen's attention to it. "Okay, sweetie, we'll get you taken care of."

Moving quickly, she draped the towel over its head, pulled it onto the dock, and held its wings against its body. She focused on the bird and fear radiated up her arms from it in the form of sharp pinpricks. So often during the years, it was fear she felt as she read the energy of a wild animal or bird. "It's okay," she whispered.

She turned to PJ. "Can you just hold him like this?" She gestured toward its body.

PJ stepped forward and reached for the bird,

"Now don't be too tentative," Gwen said. "You have to hold on to him because he's really not going to like what I'm about to do."

PJ nodded her head. "Okay." She held the bird's wings against its body.

"You're doing great," Gwen encouraged her. She lifted one side of the towel to reveal where the pelican was hooked. She concentrated on the pelican and her vision blurred for a moment as an image assaulted her – she saw the reddish goatee and chipped front tooth and the leer that had creeped her out almost her entire life. She saw her cousin, Robbie Hanes, dangling a ladyfish-baited hook in front of the pelican and laughing when the bird went after it. Then, he callously cut the line with the hook and several feet of line still engaged.

Anger seared through her. "That damned Robbie – he did this on purpose – he —" Trembling, she stopped her rant suddenly, realizing she wasn't helping to calm the frightened bird by going off. She took several deep breaths in an attempt to still her shaking hands. Then she noticed the shocked expression on PJ's face. Gwen glanced at Wyatt, who was smirking. She flushed with embarrassment.

Gwen yanked a ten-in-one tool from her back pocket. Steadying her voice, she explained what she was doing as she worked on it. "We can't just cut the line, we have to get the hook out to keep it from getting infected or caught on something else." With one hand she held the bill shut, with the other she clipped the barb off the hook and pulled it through. The bird jerked, then relaxed.

PJ smiled.

"Next, we have to untangle the line from the wing," Gwen continued. She positioned the still secured bill between her knees to hold the head still. She lifted a different section of the towel and clipped the line before unwinding it from around the wing.

"There you go," she whispered, and felt the bird relax a little more. She peeked under the towel at different places to make sure she hadn't missed any injuries. Everything else looked fine.

Gwen looked at PJ. "Okay. Now, when I say so, let go and step back." She raised an eyebrow. "Ready?"

PJ nodded.

"Now," Gwen said.

Gwen pulled the towel the rest of the way off as PJ released her hold on its wings. After hesitating for only a moment, the pelican flew to the next dock and waddled around the wood planks, repeatedly shaking its entire body and causing its feathers to ruffle.

Turning toward her brother, Gwen held up the offending paraphernalia.

"It could be anyone's," Wyatt claimed. He held out his hand and she dropped it in his palm.

"You were so great with that bird," PJ said.

"I hate seeing any pelican left to get hung up in fishing line, leaving it vulnerable to predators or starvation, but it's especially hard seeing it with these young ones," Gwen said with a shrug.

"So, that one is young?" She looked across to the other dock where the bird had settled. "How can you tell?"

Gwen gestured toward it. "See how brown its head is? An adult has a white head, with a touch of yellow."

PJ nodded. "You probably have to answer all kind of lame pelican questions around here, huh?"

Gwen cocked her head.

"Working at the marina," PJ added.

"Oh, yeah, working at the marina." She felt a surge of pleasure that the woman had noticed her, and before pulling a shotgun on her, too. Oh, yeah, the shotgun. Without a doubt, the gun was Wyatt's doing. She was going to have to talk to her brother about that stupid move.

"So, about that shotgun you almost killed me with."

PJ paled. "I am so sorry."

"Don't apologize," Wyatt chimed in. "A person has a right to protect themselves."

"Which is the argument you used when you convinced PJ she needed a gun?" Gwen asked.

"Hey, I'm just saying." Wyatt turned to PJ and cocked his head expectantly. "Got something for me?"

"Oh," Gwen said. "So, the transaction's not complete yet? Good." She stared down her brother. "I think letting her use the gun as a loaner would be an excellent show of good will."

"No, I have the–" PJ started to say.

"No, no, we insist," Gwen interrupted her. "Welcome to the neighborhood. My advice to you, however, would be not to pull that gun on someone unless you absolutely need to. Most people around here will have it turned on you in mere seconds."

PJ's eyes grew large.

"Don't worry. It's pretty safe around here." She watched as emotions flickered across PJ's face. "So, be careful with the loaner gun. And if you need anything else, I'm right over there at the ship's store."

"Yeah, and I'm around. If you need *anything*," Wyatt said.

Gwen gave her brother a little push. "Come on, help me with my kayak."

They made their way down the dock. Gwen looked back at PJ and gave a slight wave. "See you around."

"See you around," Wyatt mocked Gwen.

She elbowed him and he laughed.

"I can't believe you'd be stupid enough to sell a gun to someone you don't know. What were you thinking?"

"I was thinking she's hot and it was a good enough excuse to talk to her."

"Felons aren't allowed to be that careless," Gwen said. "You don't know anything about the woman."

"Well, first, you know that felony DUI of mine is bullshit. And second, I happen to know that she's playing for your team. And that she looked at you like she wanted to spend some time rolling around in the dugout with you."

"Shut up."

Wyatt chuckled. "So," he said. "Robbie's gonna feel the wrath of Earth Mother for hooking the flying rat?"

"What?"

"How do you figure it was him that cut the line on the pelican?"

Uneasiness rose in her gut. She walked to the slip where her kayak nestled against the dock. As she fiddled with her stuff, she felt her brother studying her. She turned to him. "What?"

His eyes narrowed as he looked her over. "Oh, little sister, I am so onto you."

"Onto me? What?"

His smile grew. "You'll see."

She rolled her eyes at him. "Want to give me a hand here? I have to get to work." She shook her head. "And cut the *little sister* crap. I'm almost thirty-eight."

†

Piper grabbed a roll of paper towels from the shelf and added it to the hand-held, plastic shopping basket with the canned peaches, several jars of soup, and a bottle of red wine.

She watched as a young boy ran up to Gwen at the counter. "I adopted a manatee," he said. "I'm in Save the Manatees and I adopted a manatee."

"You did?" Gwen exclaimed with a big smile. "That's wonderful."

"And my mom said I can buy a stuffed one. That's my mom right there."

Piper stood just close enough to hear the conversation but not be seen by Gwen.

A woman placed a stuffed manatee on the counter and smiled at Gwen. "He's been talking about nothing but manatees since we told him we were coming down to Florida for a visit."

"I'm going to name my stuffed manatee Tina," the boy said.

"Tina is a wonderful name for a manatee," Gwen said. She rang up the order and wished them a great day as the mother and son left the store.

Piper approached the counter and Gwen looked up from the computer on the desk. "Hi. PJ, right?"

"Yeah. Hi, Gwen. You've dried off."

"Doesn't take long in the sun," she gestured out the window. "Find everything you need?"

"I found some. I guess I'll need to go to a regular grocery store soon. Or maybe I'll try the restaurant."

"I'm not even sure when it's open these days," Gwen said.

"Hey, honey, someone left a mess in the men's room." The man Piper had seen talking to Gwen outside the day before hollered from the back of the store.

Piper laughed when Gwen rolled her eyes.

Gwen put all the groceries on the counter and put the basket on the floor behind her. She rang the items up and placed each in the bag, except the bottle of wine, which she placed on the floor with the hand basket.

"I can't, in clear conscience, let you buy that nasty stuff. Please wait until you go into town to get something decent. Unless you like beer. We sell enough beer that you know it's fresh."

"Maybe I'll wait," Piper said. She handed Gwen a twenty and watched her as she counted out the change. The exchange on the dock was still on her mind, and she hoped Gwen's presence near her boat was truly just about the pelican, and not a convenient ruse. She hated how paranoid she'd become, but when people want you dead, you have to be at least a little suspicious of everyone.

"So, how do you know Wyatt?" Piper asked, holding her breath, hoping Gwen didn't say they were married or dating or anything.

Gwen chuckled. "Wyatt's my brother."

Piper found herself immensely glad of that. "Your brother?"

"Yeah, but don't hold it against me."

"He seems nice enough."

"He'll do."

"What does he do for a living?"

"He's a fishing guide."

"And a gun salesman," Piper teased.

"About that," Gwen whispered. "Maybe we could keep that between us?"

Piper glanced around the store. "Don't worry. I wouldn't say anything even if you two weren't the only people I talk to."

"Thanks," Gwen said.

Piper thought about the gun, about the fear and excitement when Gwen was pushed up against her, the gun between them. Piper's fear had been so keenly mixed with excitement that for a moment she worried she might blackout. And the smoldering look Gwen gave her, albeit brief, sent butterflies to her gut and wetness to her groin.

Piper looked at Gwen from across the counter. Sandy hair peeking from under a tie-dyed bandana framed the most gorgeous green eyes Piper had ever seen. She had to have this woman.

"You okay?" Gwen asked.

"Yeah." Piper picked up her grocery bag from the counter. "I better let you get back to work." She leaned closer and said, "Especially since *someone* left a mess in the men's room."

Piper hurried from the store to the A-dock. She glanced around several times as she unlocked the door to the houseboat and slid it open. It was a lot easier now that Wyatt had shown her the secret of jiggling it. She felt a bit foolish locking the door behind her just to walk to the ship's store, but she had to keep her guard up. She put her groceries away and walked back onto the dock.

She eyed the area of the boat where she'd pulled the shotgun on Gwen. Should she take Gwen at her word? No, she couldn't take anyone at their word. Considering the predicament she was in, that could be dangerous.

She knelt on the dock and leaned over the edge to look closely at the houseboat. Nothing seemed out of order. Not that she would know, she reminded herself. She knew absolutely nothing about boats and still couldn't believe she was living on one.

She sprawled out on the dock and reached to one of the lines securing the boat. It seemed okay. She slid her hand along the boat just below the water's surface.

"Careful," Gwen purred, just above a whisper.

Piper's hand jerked out of the water and her entire body came an inch off the dock. "Damn it," she said. "Don't *ever* do that again." She rolled halfway and stopped.

"Hey, sorry," Gwen said. "But you really should be careful. I'd hate for you to lose that hand."

The way Gwen's gaze traveled the length of Piper's supine body made Piper's face heat up. Gwen stepped away and offered Piper her hand.

Piper hesitated before accepting it.

Gwen pulled her to her feet. Standing face to face, Gwen whispered in a husky voice. "I swear to the goddess that I didn't do anything to this boat this morning."

Piper's blush deepened and she broke eye contact.

Gwen cleared her throat. "I'm going into town. Why don't you come along? You can get that bottle of wine you wanted." She handed PJ a ball cap from the store, with an embroidered manatee on the front. "I brought you something."

Piper took the hat and smiled. "Thank you."

†

Tracy Snyder walked halfway down the sidewalk before she stopped and looked around. She hadn't been outside, except for short walks around the center's backyard, in three months. She turned her face up to the last of the day's sunshine and took a calming breath.

"This is the time," she whispered. "This is the time it sticks."

She looked back one last time at the rehab center's front door. She didn't plan on going back. She wasn't going to fall into bad habits again. Ever.

Making a mental note of her grocery list, she walked up to the Toyota Corolla parked at the curb. Marion, her sponsor, smiled at her from the driver's seat. "Ready?"

"Yes. Yes, I am." She climbed into the passenger seat and pulled on her seatbelt.

"We'll run by the grocery store first. Your apartment is set up with everything you'll need except for food and toiletries."

Tracy stared out the window. This really did feel like a new beginning. She smiled at the palm trees she had taken for granted most of her life.

"Remember routine is important right now. And I mean new routine, not old. Stay away from places and people who were a part of your routine when you were using," Marion said.

Tracy felt a roiling in her stomach. She had soiled her memories of some of the most beautiful places in the world. Now instead of thinking about glorious sunsets on the backwaters of the Ten Thousand Islands she would think about falling out of the Carolina skiff because she was so wacked out on oxy that she couldn't stand, let alone climb out of a boat.

"You have your list of meetings?" Marion asked.

"Yeah."

"Even though routine is important, it's okay to break it to go to extra meetings."

Anywhere, Everywhere

Tracy nodded. She looked to the right as Marion turned left onto Highway 41. They were heading away from the upscale gated community she'd grown up in, away from her mom and dad, away from the life she'd been so far removed from for so long that it no longer welcomed her.

Tracy had been such a daddy's girl when she was young. One of her fondest memories was of sitting on her father's lap and steering the family's twenty-one foot MAKO for him as they idled down the long canal that would take them to the bay and then the Gulf of Mexico. As they would leave the no-wake zone, her father would punch the throttle and she would be forced back against his muscular chest, squealing and laughing.

Then she was too old to sit on daddy's lap. And she stopped going out on the boat with the family, instead preferring the company of her friends.

And here she was, all these years later, her father financing her rehab and paying the first six months of her rent at the apartment with the stipulation that she was not to go anywhere near her family. The rent would also cease if he found out she was using again.

She turned when she felt Marion staring at her.

"You okay?" Marion asked.

"Yes. I'm fine." And she would be, with or without her family, but wasn't so sure she would make it without Wyatt. She missed Wyatt's crooked smile, the sun lightened hair hanging over his forehead, his quick sense of humor. She wanted to see him again, but not until she'd been clean for a while.

†

Gwen pushed the Publix shopping cart that she and PJ were sharing. She hung behind PJ, watching her peruse the bakery case. She couldn't help but appreciate the way her jean shorts hugged her backside, the way her calves showed off their muscle when she reached for the furthest loaf of French bread in the case. The hat she'd given her looked absolutely adorable on her, if Gwen did say so herself. She came up beside her and had to smile when PJ let out a little groan when she smelled the bread.

PJ turned to her. "Fresh bread is my weakness."

You could quickly become my weakness, Gwen mused. Then she quickly reminded herself that messing around with a tourist was not in her own best interest.

PJ placed the loaf in the back part of the cart and headed toward the meat department. Gwen hung back again, not interested in anything in the meat section. She waited while PJ studied the steak selections.

PJ approached the cart. "Do you eat meat?" she asked as she placed two packs of steaks near her loaf of bread.

"Not if it's commercially slaughtered."

"So, what kind then?"

"I have a friend who raises chickens. I get eggs from her and will occasionally take a chicken she sells me. Another friend hunts hogs and hooks me up sometimes."

"So, you're all about ethical eating, yet you advocate hunting?"

"Hunting is a lot more humane than commercial slaughtering," Gwen said.

PJ put the pack of steaks back in the meat case. "So, do you eat what Wyatt hunts?"

"Sometimes. If I believe him when he tells me he was respectful," Gwen said.

"The other day, when I got the gun from him, he asked me if I have a girlfriend."

Gwen raised an eyebrow.

"I told him not at the moment."

"Are you coming out to me?"

"Yeah, I guess I am."

"So, it'd probably put us both at ease if I just went ahead and did the same. Come out, I mean."

PJ faced her. "Yeah?"

"Yeah."

They smiled at one another.

Quit grinning like a fool, Gwen chastised herself.

"So, where are you from?" Gwen asked.

PJ hesitated. "Virginia." She made her way toward the seafood department. "So, do you eat fish?"

The quick change of subject wasn't lost on Gwen. "I'll eat locally caught fish. I want to know where it's been and whether it's been ethically caught. And that it's sustainable."

PJ nodded. She studied the groceries in her hand. "I keep having to remind myself that I have very limited refrigerator and freezer space." She put a stack of frozen dinners back into the freezer.

"That stuff's bad for you anyway," Gwen said.

"It's better than fast food. Which I notice isn't on every corner around here."

"There's more of it the farther into town you go."

"Good to know." PJ smiled. "I'm not much of a cook. I can do a decent stir-fry, but that's about it."

"Make up a batch and freeze it."

"Still there's the freezer space issue."

Gwen looked away from her. She didn't really want PJ to know her history with the boat, but couldn't keep important information from her either. "You do know there's a good sized freezer under the hatch to the bilge, right? At least there used to be."

Gwen could feel PJ staring at the back of her head. "What's a bilge?" PJ asked.

"Okay." Gwen turned to face her. "Buy whatever frozen stuff you think you need. I'll show you where that extra freezer is when we get back to *Ruffled Feathers*. If for some reason Walker has moved it, or it's not working, you can keep the frozen food in my freezer."

PJ reclaimed her TV dinners. They left the frozen section and headed toward produce.

"I know where you can get some really nice organic vegetables," Gwen said.

"If I buy some good, old-fashioned, pesticide-laden peaches will you think I'm horrible?"

Gwen stopped the forward movement of the cart. She waited until PJ turned around to look at her before speaking. "I hope you don't think I'm judgmental. Everyone has their own beliefs and I'm pretty rigid in how I live by mine, but I don't expect others to believe or act as I do."

"Sorry. I hit a nerve?"

"Wyatt's always giving me a hard time. I don't judge others, I just refuse to compromise my beliefs," Gwen said.

"Fair enough," PJ said.

"So, what do you do back in Virginia?"

"Oh, God, I almost forgot the most important reason for coming to the store," PJ said.

Another change of subject, Gwen reflected. "The wine."

"Yes, the wine."

They went to the wine aisle and Gwen watched PJ painstakingly study the selection of reds. It bothered her that PJ wouldn't tell her anything about herself. Gwen wondered if the woman even lived in Virginia. If she was lying about that, what else would she lie about?

PJ held up a bottle. "I'm so glad they have this brand. It's one of my favorites." PJ shot her a beautiful smile and Gwen almost forgave her for holding back the details of her life. She wondered, if they spent more time together, would PJ open up?

Gwen looked away from PJ and scanned the center aisle of the store. She felt like she was forgetting something, and not surprisingly, considering how distracted she got around PJ. A woman started down the wine aisle, but turned abruptly and went the other direction. For a brief moment, Gwen imagined it was Tracy, Wyatt's ex-girlfriend. She'd heard that Tracy had left Naples years ago. Besides, the Tracy she knew would never forego the wine isle.

She turned back to PJ. "I'm off the day after tomorrow," she said. "Why don't you come paddling with me?"

"Paddling?"

"Yeah, I have an extra kayak. It'll be great."

"Kayaking where the alligators are?"

"I will keep you safe. I promise."

PJ smiled. "Okay. Sounds fun."

"In the meantime, let's get back. We'll figure out your freezer options."

They stashed their groceries behind the seat of Gwen's old Ford Ranger. On the drive back, PJ pointed at a speed limit sign. "What's up with the different speed at night?"

"This is a panther zone. Since they are mostly nocturnal, the speed limit is lower at night."

"Do many get hit by cars?" PJ asked.

"Yeah. We've built condos on a lot of their habitat, so much that vehicles hitting them and intraspecies aggression is taking a hefty toll on their numbers."

They drove in silence the rest of the way to the marina and Gwen hoped she hadn't sounded too much like she was on a soap box when talking about the panthers.

Gwen held PJ's grocery bags while PJ unlocked the door to the houseboat. They went inside and Gwen placed the groceries on the counter as she glanced around. It looked the same. She fought to keep down her anger about Wyatt losing the boat to Walker. She pulled the rug from the hatch cover.

"Wow. I would have been so surprised the first time I went to bring the rug out for a shaking and saw that."

Gwen lifted the ring and pulled up on the trapdoor.

PJ craned her neck to see in. "Oh, wow. That's the freezer down there?"

"Yep. Now let's see if it still works." Gwen sat on the edge and dangled her legs over the side. She let herself drop, landing beside the freezer. "It's plugged in and turned on. Hopefully it's clean." She pulled the freezer door open. "I'll be damned. It's in good shape."

"It's useable?" PJ asked.

"Yeah." Gwen was surprised it was clean. She stared at its white walls and tried to ignore the anxiety creeping into her belly.

"Something wrong?" PJ asked, peering down at her.

"No. It's all good." She climbed back up. "You should go down and see for yourself. We need to be sure you can fetch your groceries once they're down there."

PJ lowered herself into the bilge area and looked inside the freezer. "This is great."

Gwen started to hand down a stack of frozen dinners. "You want to keep some up here?"

"Yeah." She paused. "How about the lasagna and the fajitas?"

"Okay." Gwen handed down the rest of them. "There you go." She stood back while PJ closed the freezer and climbed back up.

"I cannot thank you enough for showing me that. Do all boats have freezers down there?"

Gwen shrugged. She didn't want to tell this near-stranger her family's messed up history. Why should she? PJ wasn't telling Gwen much about herself either.

"Any other secrets about living on a houseboat I should know?"

Gwen could have gotten into things like not using too much toilet paper so the tank doesn't get full too quickly or get clogged up, but she couldn't make herself have such a conversation with this beautiful woman. She glanced into the bedroom and saw PJ's suitcase on the bed. "There's extra storage under the bed. Built-in drawers."

"Oh?"

"Yeah," Gwen felt a blush creep up her neck as she pointed to the bed. "Lift the comforter up and you'll see."

"Thanks."

"Sure."

PJ held up the bottle of wine. "I'm going to have a glass. Will you join me?"

"No, thanks. I really should be going."

"Oh," PJ said.

"My groceries are still in the truck. And I should head home."

"Well, thanks for the information on the boat. I really don't know what I'm doing here."

Gwen stared into the dark eyes and saw vulnerability. And something that looked a lot like desire. "Let me know if I can help with anything else."

"I'm good. Unless you know of a secret way for me to get Wi-Fi."

"Do you have pen and paper?" Gwen smiled at the surprise evident on PJ's face. She took the offered pen and grocery receipt and jotted down "Fishfreak101."

"Yeah?" PJ asked.

"Yeah. If you go by the hotel pool or the bench by the tennis court you'll be within range. If you decide to sit in the bar, just don't advertise that you're online via their Wi-Fi."

"Wow." PJ smiled and took a step closer. "I can't thank you enough." She reached to hug Gwen, and Gwen felt herself stiffen, then relax into the embrace.

Gwen was the first to pull away. "Good night."

"Good night."

Chapter Three

Piper walked to the edge of the trees where she could get a signal. She dialed Jeremy on her cell phone.

"Hey, Jeremy, any word on Bronson?"

"No, Piper, not a word. I mean PJ."

She watched Gwen empty one of the outside trash cans. "I bet Bronson's long gone. I could probably come home now without an issue."

"No way. You can't risk it. He's probably counting on you thinking like that. How's the laying low coming?"

"I'm bored." She watched Gwen and knew of one way to remedy that.

"Just stay alert. And don't even think about coming back here yet. Learn to fish or something."

"Ugh."

"Been online?" Jeremy asked.

"No. Why?"

"You've just had a spike in friend requests on Facebook."

"I'm not on Facebook."

"You are now," Jeremy said.

"Lord, please tell me you haven't been posting anything too embarrassing."

"I'm just posting enough to keep your *friends* interested. And to mislead Bronson's goons in case they're watching. You are just loving Seattle, by the way."

"Seattle?" Piper asked.

"Yeah, you adore the people there. And the rain."

"Good to know," Piper said.

"And when this is all over, you're going to start doing your own social networking."

"Ugh."

"All of your new friends on Facebook are lesbians. And I think I've heard you moaning and groaning with at least half of them."

"I really wish you wouldn't pretend to be me."

"You can reclaim your life when you get home. Which won't be until Bronson is behind bars. Promise?" Jeremy asked.

"I promise."

"And be careful. I've been thinking. I don't think we should talk again for a while. Just in case. I'd hate myself if they used our communication to find you and—"

"Okay. It's fine."

She stared at Gwen. That woman would be her first choice of things to occupy her time with. But she sensed she would have to take it slow with her. She swatted away an insect flying around her face. Maybe she should also get a hobby, and by hobby she meant something not involving baiting a hook or being eaten alive by bugs. "I better let you go then, Jeremy."

"I love you, Piper."

"I love you, too." She hated how final their goodbye sounded.

She took a deep breath as she walked back toward her boat. Watching Wyatt and Gwen engaged in an intense exchange, she remembered how Wyatt had joked about them not all being drug smugglers. It was time to scare up some Wi-Fi. At least she could look into the area and learn about her new neighbors' heritage to pass the time.

Piper waited outside the door of *Ruffled Feathers* to watch as Gwen and Wyatt argued. He grabbed her by the wrist in the way a brother might think he's entitled to and Gwen pulled away before giving him a little shove.

Gwen and Wyatt stood toe to toe, and even with his several inches and pounds advantage, Gwen looked mad enough to kick her brother's butt. After several moments of glaring at one another, Gwen marched to Wyatt's truck and climbed in the passenger seat.

When Wyatt pulled out, his tires made quite a statement.

"What the hell?" Piper asked herself as they disappeared.

Piper went back inside the boat and sat on the small sofa. She closed her eyes. An image of Bronson shooting the man in the head met her in the darkness and her eyes flew open again. She just wanted the images to stop.

†

When Wyatt made the right turn off highway 41 onto 29, Gwen felt the usual queasiness in her gut. A few miles down the road, she shook her head. "How can you even stand to come into this town, let alone live here?"

"I've got some damned good memories of growing up in Everglades." He gave her his lop-sided grin. "Yep. Had some good times here."

The only memory Gwen had was of betrayal and heartbreak. Bile rose up in her throat. When the police came for her father, they'd had to peel Gwen from around his legs as she screamed out. "No, don't take my daddy!"

That was July nineteen eighty three. Gwen was seven years old when her father was arrested and sentenced to five years for drug smuggling. Luke Martin never made it home.

Gwen stared out the window of Wyatt's truck as they drove into Everglades City. She fought to maintain her composure.

"Every kid should be able to grow up in a place as great as Everglades. We had the best playground imaginable in our own back yard. This place was magical – outlaws, hauling pot, and all."

"Don't do that, Wyatt." Gwen frowned at her brother.

"Do what?"

"Don't romanticize this place and that time. It's not some fun folk culture to be proud of. Lives were ruined. Lives were lost."

Wyatt dismissed her with a flick of his hand, and then pulled into Robbie's driveway. Before they got out, Gwen caught Wyatt staring at her.

"What?"

"It's nothing," Wyatt said.

"You don't stare at someone if it's nothing."

Wyatt shook his head. "Sometimes you remind me so much of mom that it kind of freaks me out." He didn't wait for a response as he climbed out of the truck. Gwen reluctantly followed him into the tiny, leaning house.

"Robbie, get lost for a few minutes."

"Hey, it's my house."

"Yeah, your filthy house," Gwen chided.

Robbie had let the house go downhill. She looked around the living room of the house where she'd been raised by her aunt and uncle, Robbie's parents. She had never felt completely at home there, but at least Robbie had moved out as soon as she moved in. The first year, while Uncle Derek was in prison, it had been just she and her aunt. Aunt Linda was the only one on the Hanes side of the family that she ever felt comfortable with.

From the age of seven to eighteen she had been fed, clothed, and sheltered in that small house. It was cramped back then, but had always been clean. When she left for the University of Florida on a full scholarship, they told her to pack all of her things – she would not be going back there, as they felt their responsibility to her was done. She could look back and realize that cutting her loose like that had been a huge favor. She had no one to fall back on so she worked hard in college and came out with a degree she could actually use…until she no longer wanted to.

"Play nice," Wyatt said. He turned to Robbie. "Just give us fifteen minutes. Then come back."

Robbie left, reluctantly.

Wyatt gestured to Gwen to follow him to the bedroom. "Seriously, Wyatt?"

"Just come on." He opened the door and stood back to let Gwen go in first. She did, then backed up, right into him.

"What the hell?" Gwen asked as she stared at several large glass aquariums. "Pythons?"

"Two Burmese and one North African Rock Python."

"Shit, Wyatt, what are you doing?"

"Python rescue. You're pretty impressed with me right now, aren't you?"

"Are you kidding me? Where did they come from?"

"One Burmese came from Picnic Key, the other one and the rock are from Big Cypress."

"As in federal lands? Without a permit?"

Wyatt shrugged.

"Oh, Wyatt, what are you into?"

"Here." Wyatt slid the top off the aquarium with one of the Burmese. "Hold this one."

"Oh, hell no," Gwen said.

He grabbed it at the base of its skull and supported its body as he lifted it out. "Hold it."

She glared at her brother but he wouldn't back down. Finally, she slid her hand up behind his to grab behind its head. Her fingertips were immediately engulfed in the pinpricks she was so familiar with when she touched a wild animal, any wild animal. She hefted its cool weightiness and sighed. "It's scared. This guy doesn't belong in a fish tank."

"What do you think about it though?"

"What do you mean, what do I think? I think you're playing with fire. What are you doing with these things?"

He took the snake from her and set it back in the tank. He turned toward the rock python.

A prickling sensation gathered at the back of her neck, then painfully shot down her back. "Don't think for a minute I'll touch that one," she said without thinking.

Wyatt reached toward the wall of the tank and the rock python struck at the glass from the other side. "Whoa," he said with a laugh.

"That snake is dangerous," Gwen said. It was not lost on her that the pain from its fierceness came without her having to touch it.

He nodded, and then pulled the other Burmese out. "Take this one."

As Gwen took the middle portion of the snake's body into her hands, its tail wrapped around her left arm, leaving a trail of light pinpricks. She closed her eyes as its head lingered in front of her face, the telltale arrowhead pattern pointing at her. She opened her eyes and the tongue flittered about, sensing its surroundings.

She concentrated on going beyond the prickly sensation. "Hey, baby," Gwen said softly.

The snake's tongue continued moving, seemingly tasting her breath, her words.

"I won't hurt you, sweetie."

"You feel something, don't you?" Wyatt asked.

Gwen moved her hand to support under the python's head. She marveled at the strength of the muscle shifting under its skin. "This girl was once someone's pet," Gwen whispered.

"And now she's being hunted," Wyatt said, his voice also low.

The snake moved to wound around Gwen's neck. Wyatt raised an eyebrow.

"She's just moving to where it's warmest. That's normal," she said. She felt a rush of empathy for this creature, felt a warming deep inside her that she could only attribute to the snake.

"Normal, huh?"

"Seriously, Wyatt," she begged. "What are you doing with these things?"

"We're rescuing them," he said. "And I want you to help us."

"It's called poaching, Wyatt."

"No."

"Robbie's selling them?"

"He's recouping our expenses."

"It's poaching. I will not have anything to do with it."

"I expected better of you, Miss I'd-risk-my-life-to-save-a-bird," Wyatt lashed out.

"That's different."

"That's fucked up. And look at you – you're skin and bones because you won't eat anything that wasn't got *respectfully*. I hope you starve on your *ethics*," Wyatt shouted.

"Screw you," Gwen retorted. She breathed deep and tried to level out her emotions. She could tell that the tension was upsetting the snake.

"No, screw you. You know killing these snakes is wrong. Now you can do something to really help."

Gwen stroked the magnificent snake. She closed her eyes and felt affection. "Where is this one going?"

"To a friend out of state. As a pet. A *cared-for* pet." He gently ran his fingertips along the length of the snake's body. "I am begging you. Just do that weird little thing you do to be sure we're rescuing the tame ones. That's all I ask. You don't have to have anything to do with any other part of this."

"How did you know?" Gwen asked.

"About you or the snake?" he teased.

"Me."

"You knew about Robbie and the flying rat." He crossed his arms. "I knew you never stopped being Dr. Doolittle. I just decided not to mess with you about it anymore."

"Don't call me that."

"Why not, Dr. Doo? You really hated it when I called you that when you were a kid."

"And I still hate it," Gwen said.

He shrugged. "But you're still talking to the animals."

"I've never *talked* to animals. Not like you mean." She hesitated, then blurted out, "I just hear them, feel their emotions."

"Can't you hear that snake asking you to save it?"

"Actually, I do." She took a deep breath. The satiny feel of the snake against her neck felt comforting. "This thing with the animals had calmed down a lot for the last ten or more years. Now, lately, it's getting strong again. Sometimes now I can even feel them without touching them."

"Why is it getting stronger?" Wyatt asked.

"I don't know."

"Well, be careful. You don't want to scare away your little girlfriend with your freak act."

"What?" Gwen asked.

"Don't play dumb. So, did the pelican tell you what the hot chick's story is?"

"Whatever it is, it's not our business," she answered. Now if she could just convince herself of that.

†

Tracy turned the car onto Highway 41, the Tamiami Trail. The Corolla Marion had loaned her was nice enough, but Tracy felt like she was sitting on the ground. She decided she'd buy a used pickup truck once she saved some money from her new job. She would become the newest hostess at Newton's Steak and Seafood the very next day. There was nothing like showing Naples' upper echelon to their tables so they could spend more on a bottle of wine than she'd make in a week, huh?

Marion had let Tracy take her car to go shopping for some comfortable shoes for her new job. The bag with the shoes sat in the passenger seat. What was one little detour into Everglades City in the big picture? She wouldn't try to find Wyatt. She wouldn't look for Robbie for drugs. No, she just wanted to prove to herself that she could go to her old stomping grounds and not be tempted.

That's what she told herself for the next twenty-five miles. When she turned south onto Highway 29, her palms began sweating. She wiped them one by one on her denim shorts.

Winding her way through town, she wasn't at all surprised when she found herself creeping past Wyatt's house. It didn't look like he was home. She wondered what he was driving these days.

Anywhere, Everywhere

Tracy meant to take a left at the stop sign but instead went right. She paused in front of Robbie's house, staring at Wyatt's old pickup truck. Was it still Wyatt's, or was it Robbie's now? She had loved that pickup, sitting close to Wyatt on the bench seat, and how he would drape his right arm across her shoulders as he drove. She had bounced down graveled, pot-holed roads with Wyatt, going to one of the free campgrounds in the Big Cypress swamp where they would party, dance around campfires, and finally make love in the back of the truck, in a borrowed tent, or on a picnic table under the stars.

Was that the last time she was truly happy? She loved nothing more than slow dancing with Wyatt in the glow of the fire, him growing hard against her and her knowing there was no place she would rather be, no one she would rather be with. At the time, she had wished she could stay in his arms forever.

Tracy jumped when the front door to Robbie's house opened. She gave the car a little gas to move mostly out of view. In the rearview mirror she saw Wyatt step out onto the porch. A woman was right behind him. She could only see a sliver of her, but it could have been Gwen. Tracy had a sharp memory of seeing Gwen at the grocery store the day she had gotten out of rehab. She hadn't been ready to face Gwen that day. It could be that she would never be ready to see Gwen's look of disappointment, or Wyatt's look of heartbreak.

But what if that wasn't Gwen? She'd been gone for five years – for all she knew, Wyatt could be married. It did kind of look like Gwen though. But Gwen had never liked or trusted her cousin. Tracy just couldn't imagine any reason why Gwen would be hanging out at Robbie's. The earth would have had to have shifted on its axis for Gwen to have anything to do with drugs, of that she couldn't have been more sure.

Tracy wondered if Robbie was still dealing.

She drove, staring at the road in front of her until she was almost out of Everglades City. Her heart was pounding and her stomach felt knotted. She knew a hit of oxy would calm her, make her hands stop shaking.

"No, no, no," she whispered. "Don't even go there in your head."

She glanced into the rearview mirror and knew the truck behind her was Wyatt's. He was far enough behind her that she could only make out the silhouette of Wyatt and his passenger. They were on opposite ends of the bench seat. There was nothing intimate about the way they sat. She felt immediate relief with that observation.

She turned off of Highway 29, onto 41, and glanced at her watch. Marion had never said she had to go right home after shopping, right?

When she passed the hotel, her face burned with shame. She had met Robbie there once when she'd run out of her prescription oxy and didn't have any money to buy any from her various other sources. She'd always run out a week or two into her monthly prescription, but that one time with Robbie, she had also ran out of money.

That had been the beginning of her rock-bottom – letting that squirrelly creep Robbie fuck her for a handful of pills – a three-day supply that she'd ended up consuming in one day in an attempt to push away the memory of Robbie touching her. She had blacked out later while driving and ended up in jail. She'd consoled herself that at least no one had been hurt. Wyatt had bailed her out. She had lied to him and said she would get help.

Tracy slammed on the brakes when a car pulled half-on and half-off the road. When she saw the passenger stick their camera out the window, she laid on the horn. "Fucking tour-iots!" She passed them just centimeters from the side of their dusty rental car. "Stupid," she muttered.

Her hands shook, and she had no doubt it was due to her memory of the hotel and not the tourists. She bypassed the turnoff for her apartment and drove to the nearest Narcotics Anonymous meeting.

Chapter Four

Gwen towed the extra orange and red kayak behind hers. She could feel her heart pounding hard, just thinking about spending time with PJ. She hoped PJ wouldn't be bored to death out on the water with her. But somehow she doubted it. Who in their right mind wouldn't love the mangrove-lined backwaters? Or so she hoped.

She smiled when she saw PJ waiting on the dock. Goodness, she was gorgeous. Gwen nodded toward the boat ramp. PJ waved and turned to make her way down the dock to follow the seawall around to the area of sloped concrete. Gwen had trouble taking her eyes off the woman's backside.

Gwen gave several hard strokes of the paddle, causing the kayak to surge partway up the ramp. By the time she hoisted herself out of the kayak, PJ was standing there waiting. Gwen's breath caught in her chest for a moment when she looked into PJ's eyes. "Hi," she finally managed to say.

"Hi, to you, too."

Gwen held up a can of bug spray. "To spray or not to spray, that is the question."

"Did you?" PJ asked.

"No. I usually wait to see how bad they are out there first. There will probably be yellow flies, maybe even a few mosquitoes since we've had some rain. But, considering the time of year, there might not be anything, either."

"Okay," PJ said, adjusting her hat. "I'll wait, too." She pulled her new ball cap lower onto her face and tucked an errant strand of hair into it.

Gwen smiled. "Then I guess we're ready?" she asked as she climbed out of the kayak.

"Yes. Are you sure I can't bring something?"

"I've got everything we'll need." Gwen untied the rope she'd used to tow the other kayak and threw it into hers. She turned both boats around to face away from the ramp. "I'll steady yours while you get in."

"I hope I can keep up with you," PJ said as she slipped on her sunglasses.

"Don't worry. We have no schedule to keep. We'll get where we're going when we get there."

"And where are we going?"

Gwen shrugged. "Wherever we end up."

"Great, I've always wanted to go there," PJ teased. She climbed in the plastic kayak while Gwen held on to the side. She laughed when it pitched slightly. "Will you still like me when you see how clumsy I can be?"

"Of course I'll still like you." She handed the paddle to her and gave her a little push, then gracefully climbed into her own kayak.

Gwen pulled up beside PJ. "The water level may be too low for us in some areas, but there should be plenty of places we can paddle. During the dry season even high tide means having to get out of the kayak and pull it across sections of the mud flats."

"When is the wet season? And is that the same thing as hurricane season? Oh crap, could we have a hurricane here?"

Gwen laughed. "Hurricane season is June through November. But we haven't had one here since Wilma in 2005."

"So I'm safe for a few months. That's a relief," PJ said.

"We've had a wet spring so far. That's why there can be some mosquitoes. And even now, after the rain we've had, the water is just high enough that we can still get places motorized boats have trouble getting."

As she paddled, she led them down the center of the canal, where there would be fewer biting flies. She'd save the aggravation of needing to swat them away for the section that would have the most bang for the buck in terms of birds and other possible wildlife.

After winding through the shallow waters, they pulled up alongside some mangroves. Surprisingly, the bugs weren't too bad. Gwen motioned toward another, nearby section of mangroves. PJ's mouth dropped open as she took in the massive numbers of birds. "Oh, my God," she whispered.

Gwen smiled. She relished the warmth that spread across her entire body at the sight of pleasure on PJ's face. She felt her body temperature rising and knew it wasn't just from the spring weather. She found herself hoping that PJ would be around in January and February when the types and numbers of birds would really soar.

PJ looked over her sunglasses. "There are a bunch of different kinds of birds in there?"

"Yeah. The white ones with the downward curving bills are ibis. The ones with the yellow feet – see there," she pointed off to the right where several birds congregated. "Those are snowy egrets. The tall white ones, great egrets."

"How about the tall grayish one there?"

"Great blue heron. One of my favorites." She gently guided PJ's kayak in the opposite direction. "That's a little blue heron."

"How about the pink ones?"

"A fan favorite," Gwen teased. "Roseate spoonbills. See how they swing their bills from side to side? That's how they feed on crustaceans, insects, frogs even, as opposed to the egrets and herons that use their dagger-like bills to snatch their lunches."

They watched in relative silence, the only sounds the occasional buzz of a fly and the shrill, far-off call of an osprey.

An engine's rumble grew closer. Voices found their way to Gwen and PJ.

"Ugh. An eco-tour." Gwen used her fingers to denote quotations when she said the word eco, a gesture she hated but still felt compelled to use in this particular case. She hoped they wouldn't flush the birds. Just then their wake came through the thin strip of mangroves and someone yelled out. "Look!"

An awkward, almost violent flurry of wings and legs filled the air. PJ ducked, needlessly, but in a manner typical of people around the large birds for the first time. Gwen sighed.

"What's that pink bird?" a shrill voice asked through the mangroves.

"It's a shovel-billed pink ibis," a man's voice boomed.

PJ looked confused and Gwen had to fight to keep from laughing out loud. Now that the tour had disturbed their serene paradise they might as well stay hidden and make the most of the entertainment.

"Will they come back?" another voice asked through the cover of the mangroves.

"Not with all the noise you guys make," Gwen mumbled.

A lone great egret remained behind. "What kind of bird is that?"

"That's a great white heron," the assumed guide said. "You can tell it apart from a great egret by how bushy its back feathers are."

Gwen cringed but resisted the urge to call the idiot out on his erroneous identifications.

"I want to see a manatee," someone shouted.

"Me, too," another voice chimed in.

And just like that, the boat and its lies chugged away.

PJ laughed. "Shovel-billed ibis?"

"Oh, my God. I've heard some absurd crap before, but that was awful," Gwen said.

There were some reputable eco-tour companies in the area, and then there was garbage like what they had just heard. Gwen felt sorry for the decent tour guides – the ones who knew their stuff and didn't harass the wildlife in the name of better tips – because they were often lumped in with the others.

"I'm no expert," PJ started, "But that's not a great white heron, is it?"

"No. It's a great egret. And the best way to tell it apart from a great white heron is by the color of its legs. Black legs means egret, yellowish means heron. So, you were paying attention."

"Of course I was."

"I was afraid I was boring the hell out of you and you were snoozing over there."

"No. Your knowledge of birds is quite fascinating. I'm so glad I have you for a tour guide. I feel dreadful for those poor folks who aren't so lucky."

Gwen found herself beaming. And blushing. "Thanks," she managed to say.

PJ swatted at a yellow fly. "Those are mean little buggers."

"Yes, they are. So, you ready to head back?"

"Yeah, I guess so." PJ looked around. "This place is a real maze."

"Yes, it is. It can be tricky to find your way out once you get in," Gwen said.

Gwen led the way, paddling at a moderate pace, keeping off to the side of PJ just enough to still see her in her peripheral vision. Back at the marina, she gave a hard paddle to propel herself halfway up the concrete boat ramp. She exited her kayak, pulled it out of the way, and waded out to

PJ's. She pulled her up the ramp several feet, and then held it steady for her. "Careful, it's pretty slick right here."

PJ balanced herself with one hand on the kayak and one on Gwen's shoulder.

Gwen couldn't help but notice how nice PJ's touch felt on her superheated skin. She followed PJ up onto the seawall.

"Thanks so much for taking me out and playing guide. And we never even saw an alligator," PJ said.

Gwen felt PJ following her gaze as she looked toward a five or six foot gator.

"Or at least I didn't see one," she added.

"It's perfectly safe," Gwen said.

"I believe with you, it is," PJ said as she gave Gwen a big smile.

"Anytime you want to go back out there, just give me the word."

"Okay." PJ shuffled her feet, making Gwen smile.

A few flies found them and Gwen watched as PJ swatted at them. "I'd better let you go," Gwen said. "Don't want the bugs to scare you away from going paddling with me again."

Gwen sat in the kayak and floated while she watched PJ walk along the seawall toward the dock where *Ruffled Feathers* was secured. She started to paddle when she had an idea. She pulled alongside the dock just as PJ was approaching the boat.

"Why don't I just tie this kayak to the dock right here and that way you can go out anytime you feel like it?"

PJ bit her lip. "I wouldn't dream of going out there without you."

"So, then I'll tie it up so we have it available anytime *we* decide to go out there."

"That would be great," PJ said.

As Gwen paddled away, she glanced back at the splash of orange and red color against the muted brown of the dock. She liked how it looked. She liked the implications – seeing PJ again.

Movement to her left caught her attention. A tourist was trying to flag her down from the end of the C-dock. She considered ignoring him, but she saw something that didn't look right in the water below where he was standing and frantically waving his arms.

"Crap, what now?" she asked herself as she paddled toward the C-dock.

"I think something is wrong with this manatee," the guy called out to her.

The creature was obviously struggling to submerge itself, and was barely keeping its head out of the water. It probably had air trapped inside it from a punctured lung. That was a common problem with manatees who'd been hit by boats. She let her kayak drift close to it. She looked up at the guy. "This is never okay for you to do, okay?"

He gave her a questioning look. She reached out and placed her hand against the exposed back. She could barely feel the pinpricks on her palm. She got a sense of lethargy and hopelessness.

She noticed a series of scars from past encounters with boat propellers. This time it was probably the hull of a speeding boat that struck her, breaking her ribs, causing them to puncture her lung.

Gwen pulled out her cell phone and called the Florida Fish and Wildlife hotline. She gave the operator her name and location, as well as a quick assessment of the manatee's probable injuries. She was assured someone would be right there as they had an officer in the area already and it wouldn't take long.

"Can you stay with it until he comes?" the voice on the line asked.

"Of course." She discontinued the call and repositioned her kayak closer to the manatee's head. She reached out and pulled the exhausted head onto her kayak with one hand, holding the side of the dock with the other.

"Can I help?" the visitor asked.

"Sure. Would you mind going to the driveway by the store back there and waiting for the FWC truck? That way they won't waste any time trying to find us."

He nodded his head and took off.

Less than five minutes later, Duane Shivers pulled up in his boat. A woman was with him, someone Gwen recognized as a biologist with the FWC.

"Are they sending a truck, too?" Gwen asked.

"Yeah. It will be here in a few minutes," Duane answered. "What do we have going on?"

"My guess is a punctured lung. Looks like there is air trapped, keeping her from submerging all the way." Gwen nodded her head toward the mammal. "She's exhausted."

"We can start moving her toward the ramp so she's ready for the team when they get there." He turned to the biologist. "You want to help Gwen with her while I drive? Get the rope around the manatee and then lean far enough to help Gwen keep her head up."

Anywhere, Everywhere

"You better not dump me in the water again, dude," the biologist said.

He laughed. "I promise to try my best to keep it slow and steady."

They got the rope positioned around the manatee and Gwen let Duane's boat push her kayak as she and the biologist held onto the manatee's head.

"I'm Mandy," the woman said.

"Gwen. Nice to meet you, just sucky circumstances."

"Yep."

Gwen glanced toward the ramp and saw that the truck had already backed up to it. Three women and one man were waiting with a stretcher that wasn't much more than a blue tarp stretched between two white poles. The visitor who had flagged her down stood just a few feet off to the side.

When they got to the boat ramp the techs brought the stretcher down as far as they could. Duane, Mandy, and Gwen brought the manatee to it.

"What shall we name this one?" one of the techs asked.

"Isla?" another responded.

Gwen knew that they usually nick-named the rescues after where they were found.

"We already have Isla I, II, and III. They hit a lot of manatees around here, you know," the third woman chimed in.

"You the one who found her?" Duane asked the visitor.

"Yes, sir."

"What's your name?"

"Chris Colton."

"Okay, let's get CC up into that truck so she can get on her way to the hospital."

Chris helped the rest of them carry the manatee on the stretcher up the ramp and into the truck. The three women got in back with the manatee and worked to keep her skin moist. Gwen was pretty sure Chris had tears in his eyes as the truck pulled away with its patient.

Duane scanned the small crowd that had gathered to watch. "That manatee was hit by a boat, most likely one that was speeding. That's why it is so important to follow the laws and to not speed in manatee zones. That and because if I catch you, I'm writing you a big old ticket." With that last part, he winked at Gwen.

"Thanks, Duane," Gwen said. She was so glad not to have to be the one to engage in the teaching moment that time. She was growing weary of always being the one to point out why people shouldn't do the stupid things they did.

"You did good," Gwen said to Chris.

He smiled. "I was supposed to go fishing with my buddies. The boat left me when I was late getting here."

"I bet you'll have a much more interesting story to tell than they will."

"Yes." He rocked on his feet a little. "Do you think she'll be okay?"

"I hope so."

Duane handed Chris his card. "Call me in a few weeks and I'll give you an update on CC."

Gwen got back in her kayak and looked toward *Ruffled Feathers*. She smiled as she saw PJ standing just outside the doorway to the boat, watching.

Chapter Five

Piper sat at a high-top table in the corner of the bar. She surfed the internet while nursing a glass of chardonnay. The grocery store wine was better – and much cheaper – but at least sitting in the bar she could get more comfortable than she did trying to work on her laptop on the stiff bench by the tennis court. She felt on high-alert with the few people coming in and out of the bar though. She was glad to be in a corner with a wall to her back, ensuring no one could see her laptop screen and she was able to see everyone who came in.

She closed her eyes briefly and the image of Bronson shooting the man in the head assaulted her. She wondered if she would ever be rid of that vision.

She took a sip of her wine and glanced up as a man in shorts and a fishing shirt came in and plopped on a bar stool. She was careful not to make eye contact. She didn't want to encourage any conversation.

Piper clicked on a link for news in the Everglades. It had taken her a while to catch on that folks used the term *Everglades* to mean everything from Everglades National

Park to the Big Cypress Swamp, Ten Thousand Islands, and several state and federal parks and forests.

Time would pass more quickly if she engaged her mind on something other than wondering how much longer she'd have to hide out. She typed in *News* and *Everglades City* into the search engine. There had been a bar fight in Everglades City the weekend before. She didn't care much about that, so she kept looking. Halfway down the page she found several articles about the nineteen eighties and drug smuggling. Her eyes darted around her computer screen, around the bar, and back to her screen. She had to be vigilant. It could be deadly to get caught up in what she was researching and not see Bronson or one of his goons coming.

She read about Saltwater Cowboys. Her stomach churned as she imagined how heartless the smugglers would have to have been to just dump living cows off a boat into the gulf to drown just so they could off-load the drugs hidden below deck. The image didn't mesh with the few people she'd met so far. Okay, so she'd only gotten to know Gwen and Wyatt, but couldn't imagine anyone being that heartless.

She was curious about how most of the articles tended to come to the defense of the smugglers, justifying their actions as misguided reactions to a heavy-handed government restricting their fishing, therefore their ability to make a living.

The first big bust happened in nineteen eighty three. *Operation Everglades*. At the time it was a really big deal in its scope and size. She wondered how old Gwen would have been then. She wondered if it had affected her life.

Most of the articles claimed it touched every family in Everglades City to some extent. Most of the adult male population was arrested at one point or another. Did that include members of Gwen's family?

She couldn't immediately find any listing of those arrested, but figured if she dug enough she'd come up with it. Did she really want to know if Gwen's family was involved in drug smuggling? Did it matter if they were, considering it was all history?

She clicked on a few more links and learned that there was a new drug problem in Everglades City. Prescription painkiller abuse was at near epidemic proportions according to one exposé. A new generation was getting into a new way of doing business. Wyatt and Gwen would never be involved in something like that, right?

No, not Gwen. There was no way Gwen was involved in anything illegal or immoral. *No way*, she thought, mentally closing the subject. She might not have known Gwen for long, but she was certain that the woman was honest. And she knew Gwen was ethical, especially when it came to food harvesting.

Piper typed Joseph Bronson's name into her search engine. A slew of options trailed down her screen.

She minimized the screen as the bartender approached her.

"Can I get you another wine?"

Piper swirled what was left around her glass. "No, thanks. I'll take an iced tea. Are you serving food?"

"Yes. Would you like to see a menu?"

"No, that's okay. How about a chicken sandwich and fries?"

She waited until the bartender had gone back to the bar and started keying her order into the computer before pulling her search results back up. The skin on her arms crawled as she read the first headline. "Suspected Mob Murderer Still on the Run."

She read through the article, nothing new there. The next article, however, stopped her cold. The last paragraph described how Piper Jackson, an area photographer, was also on the run, presumably for her life. Seeing her name in print made her more than a little nauseated. She closed out of that and went back to her Everglades City research.

As her sandwich was delivered to her table, she minimized her screen again. She took a few bites, and then thought about Gwen and her ethical eating. Was this chicken's life and death humane? She took another bite and struggled to swallow it. She decided to stick to the fries. If there were any ethical issues with potatoes, she didn't want to know about it.

She pushed her plate away and went back to her laptop. Another article informed her that additional drug busts occurred during the nineties as well. Did people never learn from their mistakes?

Hell, had Piper learned from hers? Probably not. If there wasn't the very real threat of Bronson hunting her down and killing her, she would be in Everglades City snooping around for a new smuggling story.

Or would she? If she found out tomorrow that Bronson and all of his men were in prison and the hit was no longer out on her, would she start on something else with the potential to be dangerous? What if it had the potential to show her a side of Gwen or Gwen's family that she'd rather not know?

Anywhere, Everywhere

†

Tracy came home from her Narcotics Anonymous meeting and popped two ibuprofen tablets. The pain meds did little to help the pain in her knee, but she didn't dare consider anything else, even under the care of a physician who knew about her addiction.

She made herself a sandwich and sat to eat it. The meeting she'd attended earlier made her feel a strange combination of desperate and hopeful. She didn't know how to explain it, and surely didn't like the feeling. But she was making sobriety work for her and that was all that mattered.

She bit into the turkey and Swiss. There was no comparing it to the food they served at Newton's, where she worked. The amount of money people spent on dinner there was staggering. Okay, she admitted, she'd spent more than that on partying when she had the funds. It wasn't something she was proud of, but she also refused to hide from her past. She had to come to terms with it if she was going to win the battle against addiction.

She cleaned up after her lunch and jumped into the shower. She stayed a long time. The worst part about the rehab center was that they had limited time allowed in the shower. They said it was to allow enough hot water for all of the residents, but Tracy was not convinced that it wasn't their way of having a power trip.

Tracy stepped out of the shower, swiped at the condensation, and then stared at her reflection in the mirror. She took a deep breath. "You are a kind, loving person. You are deserving of love and kindness. Your inner beauty shines brightly. You are strong."

She examined herself. She'd gained a few pounds while in rehab, but could live with that. Her face had been so gaunt while she was using that she'd grown accustomed to that look, but knew she looked better to the rest of the world with features less sunken.

She closed her eyes and saw Wyatt's face.

"You are worthy of forgiveness," she said to herself as she opened her eyes again. She wondered if she'd ever be able to convince Wyatt of that.

She smiled at the memory of first meeting Wyatt. They'd met at a football game at her high school. He was nineteen, two years older. He was going through a rough time, she'd found out later, because his dad had just died while in prison. Tracy found it exciting to date someone from Everglades City, someone whose family had been busted for smuggling marijuana, or as Wyatt put it, hauling pot.

Tracy's daddy didn't approve of Wyatt, no big surprise, and made it pretty hard for her to be with him. She and Wyatt had drifted apart, and it wasn't until several years later when he'd walked into the bank where she worked that they'd got serious about dating. Tracy would never forget the look the others in the bank gave him when he walked in wearing white, rubber, knee-high crabber boots with dirty jeans, and a torn T-shirt. When he recognized her, he smiled. And the warmth in her body spread just like the slow, crooked smile that was vintage Wyatt.

He ended up going to the teller two down from Tracy and she wasn't at all surprised at the end of the day when he was outside waiting for her in the parking lot, showered and shaven. He was the most handsome man she'd ever seen. She'd walked up to him and smiled.

"Would you like to go somewhere and talk?" Wyatt had asked her.

"I would love to," she'd answered.

"Where to?"

"Anywhere and everywhere," she had answered with a huge grin.

†

Gwen glanced toward the hotel as she left the ship's store. She'd seen PJ carry her laptop in that direction earlier in the morning. She hoped the Wi-Fi code she'd given PJ worked okay. She couldn't help but wonder what type of stuff she was looking up online. Was she conducting business? Was she emailing a girlfriend? Hell, there was no telling, especially since PJ wasn't telling her anything about herself.

Halfway to the boat ramp, Gwen saw that her brother already had her kayak on his Boston Whaler. She'd been hoping that the darkening sky to the west would make Wyatt change his mind about going out. No such luck. She resigned herself to just do it – just get it done. She sighed when she saw that Robbie was already on the boat. He held a plastic soda bottle up to his mouth and spit his snuff junk into it. She cringed.

"Okay, little sister, let's rock and roll."

"I don't know why she's got to come," Robbie muttered. He turned to the manatee zone sign to the side of the boat ramp and spit on it.

"Because the feds love her and they'll stop us a million times before we make it back to the marina." Wyatt turned away, dismissing their cousin. He looked at Gwen and winked.

Gwen understood that Wyatt was keeping her confidence. She hoped she could come out of this python thing with her empathy secret intact and no charges brought against her for poaching snakes. She hated that she felt compelled to help the pythons, whereby also helping Wyatt and Robbie.

She looked at Robbie and her skin crawled. "Just this once," she whispered to her brother.

Wyatt laughed, this time dismissing Gwen. "Time to go."

Gwen slipped into her life vest, even though the guys chose not to. The law said they had to have them on the boat, not that they had to wear them. Wyatt and Robbie were each sitting on their Coast Guard mandated personal floatation devices as they puttered through the no-wake zone.

"This speed limit's ridiculous," Robbie complained. "Damned manatees don't even belong here."

Gwen was surprised when Wyatt beat her to the correction. "Yes, they do. Don't be stupid."

The manatees had been around that area longer than people, but Robbie had been listening to self-serving liars wanting to justify being careless around the manatees for so long that if she'd said anything to that effect, he'd just blow her off.

"I ain't stupid," Robbie argued, in his usual, not very expressive or articulate way. "Next you'll tell me there ain't no such thing as black panthers."

Gwen groaned. She kept her retort to herself though, knowing that no matter how many facts say otherwise about no documented cases of Florida panthers with melanistic qualities, he would never believe her or anyone else.

Gwen looked up at the sky and saw the dark mass of clouds had dissipated. Just her luck, no storm when she wanted one.

"How did you get the rest of the day off today?" Wyatt asked her.

"Herb wanted the day off tomorrow so we traded."

They both looked when Robbie cast his line into the water. "What?" he asked. "Might as well fish while we inch our way down the canal."

Wyatt turned back to Gwen. "So Herb traded a half day for a full one, huh? Typical."

Oh, you just don't know. "Oh, well," she said. "I'd still rather be dealing with that letch than stuck in an office crunching numbers all day."

"Now, that's my little sister. When you came out of college with a degree in accounting I thought I'd lost you for sure."

She looked away. He always made his comments about their past so casually. She could only assume he did so because he hadn't a clue how devastating it'd been for her to be taken away from their home and thrown into the dark, back bedroom at her aunt and uncle's. They'd done the best they could for her, but having to live years as the tolerated orphan in Robbie's parent's house was dreadful. The court wouldn't let the seven year old live with Wyatt at first because of his age, then because of his DUIs.

"Okay, here is good," Wyatt said.

Robbie killed the engine and let the boat drift a little.

Gwen helped Wyatt lower the kayak out of the boat. She went into the water first, then he handed her several pillowcases and a large, black trash bag. She put them on the seat with the life vest she had pulled off and swam the kayak toward the edge of the island. It was shallow enough to walk, but she didn't know what she'd step on and preferred not to find out. Wyatt slid into the water with a long stick and swam past her.

Gwen watched as Wyatt hoisted himself onto the outer edge of the mangrove roots. He was barefoot and the way his toes curled around the prop roots as he scurried his way to them reminded Gwen of why she used to tease him about his monkey feet.

Two wood storks took flight, clumsy and awkward, a riot of black and white feathers and pink legs.

"We shouldn't be out here. We shouldn't be disrupting the birds." Wyatt couldn't hear her, but she had to say the words anyway.

As she grabbed a branch and pulled herself up, she looked down at her own feet, clad in an old pair of hiking sandals. She picked her way across the mangrove roots and the way they gave under her weight made her think about walking on plastic clothes hangers. Not a particularly pleasant sensation.

She was relieved when her feet hit the solid support of the oyster shells making up the island's interior. A lot of the islands were nothing but mangroves growing out of oyster bars, so she was glad this one had some bare ground to stand on. Her relief dissolved when Wyatt reached into a tangle of mangrove roots.

Without saying a word, Wyatt jerked out his hand. She'd barely registered his movement when she saw he had a very large snake by the tail.

"You didn't waste any time," Gwen mumbled. Her brother had an uncanny ability to track anything. It's what made him a great fishing and hunting guide, but also what made Gwen think maybe Wyatt was more like her than he would admit to himself, let alone anyone else.

The snake tried to go farther into the roots, but Wyatt pulled it back out. It lunged with its mouth opened and hissing. Wyatt released the tail just long enough to maneuver out of reach of the python's bite, then snatched it up again.

Wyatt and the snake repeated the dance for almost half an hour before the python showed any sign of tiring out.

"Hand me my stick," he instructed Gwen. She looked around the ground until she saw his bamboo walking stick. She handed it to him.

"Come on, buddy, don't you get me." Wyatt whispered, the stick in one hand and the snake's tail in the other,

"You want the pillowcase?" Gwen asked as she eyed it on the ground behind Wyatt and worried that it wouldn't be big enough for the huge reptile.

"I really don't think this thing is pet-quality." Right after speaking, he used the stick to press down the snake's head. He kneeled beside it and grabbed it right behind its jaw. "Feisty one."

Wyatt stood up with the snake's head safely immobilized. The snake's heavy body writhed in the air, then it tried to wrap around Wyatt's arm. Her brother untangled it with his free hand. He jumped and groaned when the snake defecated, some of it getting on Wyatt's arm and leg. His grip on the head never altered.

"Not nice," he hissed. Gwen knew it was a defensive measure and had to work hard not to laugh at the look of disgust on Wyatt's face.

"It don't take no Dr. Doolittle to know this one's mean as hell." He looked at Gwen. "But come touch its body and tell me what it tells you."

Gwen looked for a place on the snake not covered with bodily waste and wrapped her fingers around the snake's girth. Pinpricks assaulted her hand and arm, causing her to become uneasy. There was definitely no pet-vibe. She felt nothing but wildness – at least twelve feet of wildness and insatiable hunger. In these islands that was a disastrous combination.

"I wouldn't have it as a pet," she finally said. The pinpricks grew in intensity until they were stabbing pain. Its body lashed through the air, as if in response to her. She let go, having felt one last surge of aggression from it.

"Very bad news, isn't it?" Wyatt asked.

"I still can't believe they are out here in the salt water." She glanced around. "Even if it is pretty brackish throughout this area with all the rain the past few years."

"More and more is being said about their tolerance," Wyatt said. "People don't know shit about adapting."

"I guess I just hoped they wouldn't expand their range."

Wyatt placed his hand with the snake's head on the ground, and then traded his hand for his foot. Gwen turned away, reflex taking over, when she saw Wyatt pull out the machete that had been sheathed at his side.

Even without seeing the act, Gwen knew Wyatt had decapitated it. Anger raged through Gwen. "Wyatt!"

"What the hell did you think I was going to do, kiss it and let it go?"

She couldn't look at it. She knew logically... She stared, focusing on the mangrove's prop roots, trying to reconcile her respect for all creatures, but knowing that these predators were destructive to the entire ecosystem.

"Look, Gwen," Wyatt demanded. She turned to see what he was doing just as he sliced it open. "Look at this." He loudly counted off the bird eggs inside. "Twenty one eggs and this thing."

"That *thing* is a clapper rail." Gwen looked at the eggs. They were creamy white with some irregular brownish blotches. The right coloring and size for a clapper rail's eggs. And since there were so many of them, multiple broods. She glanced at the adult rail's body. Just like that, two generations gone.

She took a deep breath. It was bad enough that the rails were prey to hawks, harriers, and even raccoons, but now they had to worry about invasive snakes as well.

Wyatt extended the incision on the python's belly. "And a wood stork, Gwen."

She looked away, feeling sick about the implications of the protected species in the snake's stomach. A coldness settled in each place she'd felt the stabbing sensations earlier. She'd never felt anything like that before.

"This is a freaking eating machine, Gwen. What about all your wildlife?"

He was right. She'd read about what the invasive snakes had done to the population of small mammals in

Everglades National Park and sure didn't want that to happen here. But still... "Cutting its head off isn't a really humane way to kill it."

"Sorry, but I don't have a drill to scramble its brains. I'm not sure that's even a better way," Wyatt said. He placed it in the black trash bag.

Gwen lagged behind, still angry, as they headed back toward the boat. When they saw that the FWC was pulled up beside Robbie talking to him, they kept their distance. After the FWC left, they continued toward the boat.

"This is where you come in. Fish and Wildlife stops us all the time."

"Gee, Wyatt, I wonder why," she said.

Wyatt waved her comment off. "So, if you have the goods with you in the kayak..."

"Why don't you just leave the dead one out here? The vultures will take care of it. Or throw it in the water. You only really need to take out the living ones that were once pets."

Wyatt rolled his eyes. "Because me and Robbie make money on the skins."

"You're nothing but a poacher. Admit it."

"Call it what you want. What's really important here is that we're saving the domesticated ones. We're rescuing them."

"This is illegal and you're going to get us all into trouble." She grabbed her paddle and positioned the kayak at the edge of the water. When she got in, Wyatt put the sack with the dead python into the back storage compartment. "Just this once, Wyatt. I swear."

"We'll see you back at the marina."

Anywhere, Everywhere

She paddled along the edge of the mangroves, trying not to think of the dead snake behind her. Forty minutes later, she saw that the same FWC agent, Duane Shivers, had Robbie and Wyatt stopped. If they were stopped any more, she might beat them back to the marina. She looked straight ahead as she paddled past.

†

Piper watched as Gwen paddled up to the dock farthest from hers. Wyatt was waiting there for Gwen and she handed him what appeared to be a black trash bag half full of something. Piper immediately thought of the smuggling.

When Gwen turned her kayak away from Wyatt and paddled in Piper's direction, Piper's heart raced. She had to pretend she didn't see the hand-off. Were Gwen and Wyatt the new breed of drug smugglers plaguing Everglades City and the surrounding areas? Were they dangerous? Were the people they were working with dangerous?

As Gwen came closer, Piper saw her face morph into a smile. At that distance she couldn't see Gwen's eyes yet, but knew that they were sparkling. Piper had never seen a mouth and eyes tag-team a smile in such a glorious way until she'd met Gwen.

Piper forgot all about her worries concerning Gwen's possible smuggling as the kayak coasted up to where she stood on the A-dock.

"Hi," Gwen said.

"Hi, yourself." She felt like she was the breathless one even though it had been Gwen exerting herself with the paddle.

"You busy?" Gwen asked.

Piper laughed at the absurdity of her being busy.

"You know – now that you're online and all." She squinted. "You did get on with the Wi-Fi, didn't you?"

"Yes, thank you so much for that. And no, I'm not busy."

Gwen shifted her body in the kayak. "I'm a little tired of sitting. Would you like to go for a walk with me?"

"I'd love to. Just let me double-check that I locked the door to the boat."

"I'll meet you by the boat ramp."

Piper watched as Gwen paddled away, aware that she had a huge grin on her face, and then she rushed to check the door of the boat.

When Piper caught up with Gwen, she studied the fishing shirt Gwen wore over her tank top. There should be a law against covering up shoulders like hers, Piper thought.

Piper's stomach gave a little flutter when Gwen took her by the hand. Then she realized it was just to steer her in a wider arc away from a vulture on the side of the road, next to the guard rail. Gwen released her hand and the void left behind on her skin felt wrong. Piper looked closer at the bird. Its bald, black head was bent forward and she realized there was a dead vulture under the guard rail.

"It's like he's saying a eulogy," Piper commented about the way it stood above its fallen comrade.

"Or grace," Gwen countered.

When Piper's laugh erupted out of her, the vulture took two hops sideways, away from the women.

"Sorry." She apologized to the bird. She noticed Gwen smile and remembered the first time she'd seen her from a distance she'd been talking to a pelican.

Gwen's smile broadened and she gave Piper a little bump, shoulder to shoulder.

"Why do some vultures have red heads and some have black?" Piper asked.

"Black vultures always have black heads. Turkey vultures have red heads except when they're young, then their heads are dark enough to be confused with black vultures."

"So, you might think one is a black vulture but it's really a young turkey vulture?"

"Yeah," Gwen said. "But the way you can always tell the difference is that the black ones have white patches on the tips of their wings."

"Between the males and females being different and the young ones, too, I don't think I'll ever learn my birds."

"So, to tell you now about the different species' seasonal plumages would only discourage you?"

Piper laughed. "I'd love to hear all about it, even if it doesn't stick. I could listen to you talk about birds and things all day long." As soon as she said it she felt the color rise on her cheeks.

They walked along the well-manicured lawns of neat homes lining a grid of canals. The desire to take Gwen's hand or to pull her in for an embrace was getting stronger and stronger with each step they took.

"Hey, PJ, look up."

She did. And saw a large, black and white bird with a deeply forked tail soaring above them. "Oh, that is gorgeous."

"Swallow-tailed kite." Gwen pivoted around as she spoke, tracking the bird as it made a wide, smooth arc in the air. "My first kite for this year. They're my favorite bird. Well, them and kingfishers. Oh, and great blue herons."

Piper laughed. "They are all your favorites, aren't they?"

"I guess my favorite is what I'm watching at that moment." She stopped and looked at Piper.

Piper studied the green eyes that said more than Gwen had ever let her words say. Gwen wanted her – hell, Gwen *liked* her – even if she didn't say it. Of this, Piper was becoming more and more confident.

Gwen was the first to look away. "It's getting dark over that way," she said as she looked up at the sky. "At least so far the weather's been okay for you on the boat."

"The first day I was here there was a huge storm. Scared the crap out of me. Then afterward I watched you paddle home from work. And that made it worth it."

"Well, then, glad I could help out in some way." A rumble echoed. "We should head back to the marina."

"Okay," Piper said. But they didn't hurry there. They paused on the way to the dock where *Ruffled Feathers* awaited. The sky was dark in one direction, but the sun was still shining on the center part of the slips, causing the white parts of the boats to look like they were glowing.

"It's beautiful, isn't it?" Gwen said in a near whisper.

"Yes," Piper whispered back. It suddenly was too bright, too beautiful for her to keep looking at, so she looked down. She wanted to look at Gwen but she too, was too beautiful at that moment. She used the toe of her shoe to play with some disk-like things sprinkled throughout the edge of the seawall next to the fish cleaning station.

"Fish scales," Gwen explained.

Piper quit pushing them around with her shoe. "Oh." She tried not to look too prissy around Gwen but was pretty sure Gwen knew she was a bit grossed out.

They headed off again and quickened their pace when a streak of lightning lit up the sky. "Good thing it's not the rainy season," Piper teased.

Gwen laughed. "Oh, you haven't seen anything yet." Large, fat drops of rain started down as soon as they approached the dock. "Careful, the dock gets slippery in the rain."

They hurried down the dock and Piper couldn't hold back a smile when she realized Gwen was coming to the boat with her. She did a mental scan of the inside and was glad she'd cleaned up the dishes and put away the notes she'd taken on Operation Everglades earlier in the day.

She fumbled a little with the key and allowed Gwen to help when she offered. They went in and Piper flipped on a light.

"How's the freezer doing?" Gwen asked.

"It's great. Sometimes there are weird noises, but it's okay."

"Want me to take a look at it while I'm here?"

"No, that's all right. It's probably just me being hyper-aware," Piper said.

"Hyper-aware, huh?"

Piper smiled. "Yeah." She wanted to tell Gwen why she was so paranoid. She wished she could describe to her what she saw so often when she shut her eyes and the image of the man shot in the head invaded her thoughts.

She didn't want to think of that at that very moment. She would much rather study every inch of Gwen's face. She wanted so badly to kiss Gwen. She closed the distance between them and leaned forward... then jumped at a huge flash of lightning and clap of thunder.

"Wow," Gwen said. "That was right on top of us." She pulled the curtain above the dining table to the side and peered out. "Do you have any electronics on that you should unplug?"

"No. You should probably wait this out here, right?"

"Would that be okay?"

"Absolutely." Piper knew her smile must be absurdly large.

Gwen leaned against the counter and ran her fingertips along the trim of the cabinet. It wasn't until Piper had followed the movement for several moments that she realized Gwen was tracing the curve of a heron's neck. Piper couldn't believe she'd not noticed the images of birds carved along the trim before then.

"I'm glad you came by."

"So am I," Gwen said.

"I learned something about vultures and saw a new bird. That kite was gorgeous." She'd seen a movie with Jeremy and Anthony about birders. "Do you keep a list of birds that you've seen?"

Gwen laughed as she tapped her finger against her temple. "Just in here."

"So if I started a list would you think I'm a dork?" Piper asked.

"Not at all. I would think you're pretty cool."

"I don't think I've ever been considered cool. Not even for a minute."

"So, what do you do for a living?" When Piper didn't answer, Gwen crossed her arms. "It's not a hard question, PJ."

"I – ah – I'm a wedding photographer," Piper said, looking away.

Gwen studied her. "When you hesitate before answering any question I ask, or change the subject constantly, it makes it look like you're keeping something from me."

Piper just shrugged. She wished Gwen would just shut up and kiss her instead of playing twenty questions all the time. Piper's gaze remained on Gwen's fingertips, now tracing a carved pelican. She didn't want to look at Gwen, didn't want Gwen to see how scared she was to share even the tiniest detail of her life as long as Bronson was out there, hunting her. "There's nothing to tell."

"Give me something, PJ. Please."

She could tell Gwen was struggling with something, but couldn't let down her guard. "There's nothing…" Piper gave what she hoped came across as a playful shrug. "What you see is what you get?"

"Well, then." Gwen propelled her body away from the counter. "Looks like the storm is passing. I better get going."

Piper knew better than to stop her.

†

Tracy scanned the shelves of lightbulbs at Lowe's. When had there become so many kinds? Not that she'd ever bothered before. She'd gone right from her dad doing everything for her to Wyatt doing most things that would involve a trip to the hardware store.

She stopped her perusal when she could feel someone watching her. She knew who would be standing there before she turned around. She couldn't *not* turn around.

The lightning fast series of emotions that crossed Wyatt's face was dizzying. She could recognize surprise and disappointment and anger. And maybe love? Maybe he still had a small place in his heart for her even after all that she'd done?

"Hi, Wyatt."

He nodded his head slowly. "Hey, Tracy."

They stood there staring at one another until a man pushing a flatbed cart needed to get past them. When they both stepped aside, it brought them several feet closer to one another.

"You look good," Tracy said. She hoped he wouldn't try to be nice and say she did too because it would have been a lie. She looked exactly how you'd expect someone to look after being in and out of rehab much of their adult life.

"How you doing?" Wyatt asked.

"I'm okay." And she was. She truly believed she was.

He just nodded. Tracy could tell he was at a loss for what to say to someone who'd lied to him, cheated on him, and stole money from him when she was desperate for 'just one more pill.'

She looked away.

"I guess I should get back to shopping." Wyatt nodded toward the light bulbs. "You need some help with that?"

She wanted to tell him yes. She wanted to tell him so many things. But the words wouldn't work. She shook her head.

"Okay, then. Guess I'll see you around," Wyatt said as he backed away from her.

"Yeah, that would be nice." She watched as he turned and left the store. It dawned on her that he hadn't finished his shopping and that maybe he was as affected by seeing her as she was seeing him.

She grabbed a three-pack of the bulbs that looked the most like what was in her apartment. She could always return them if they were the wrong ones.

As she paid for her bulbs she glanced up just in time to see Wyatt's truck pass by the window. She knew it would be hard to see him the first time. The tightness in her chest reaffirmed that.

All she could think about now was seeing him again. She hoped that the awkwardness would be restricted to just that first, surprise encounter. Next time he wouldn't be so shocked. She didn't know if that was a good thing or bad. What if next time he was ready to tell her exactly how badly she'd screwed him over. Maybe the next time he wouldn't be so civil. She wouldn't be able to wait too long to see him again. Only then would she know how he would react to seeing her.

She drove back to her apartment, thinking about how much she wished she could turn back the clock. She wished she could go back to that day when she and Wyatt were partying, when they'd gotten into the back of his pickup truck, drunk, and started dancing to some song she'd long since forgotten.

She'd been dancing in the bed of his truck, enjoying the way her movements seemed to entrance Wyatt. She loved him so much, loved being the reason for that passionate look on his face. It was while she was watching him watch her that she slipped. She heard the pop in her knee and knew she was in for some serious pain. She let Wyatt help her down from the truck but wouldn't let him take her to the emergency room.

The next morning when she'd woken up her knee was three times its normal size and shooting pain up and down her leg. Wyatt had woken up and looked at her knee. "What the hell did you do?" he'd asked.

She had shrugged and pretended she didn't know what had happened either.

She called in sick to her job at the bank and went to the walk-in clinic. The doctor prescribed oxycodone and gave her very specific guidelines for taking the time-released pill every twelve hours. She let Wyatt drive her home. He dropped her off because he had some business to attend to at the marina. She took the pill and snuggled into the couch. Twenty minutes later, a slow smile crept onto her face as the sense of euphoria enveloped her. The pain had disappeared.

She followed the dosing to the letter for the first two weeks. Then it started to change for her. She could vividly remember that moment, when she started shaving a few hours off the time between doses, then the thought came to her that if one pill made her feel so good, two would make her feel even better. The euphoria was just as potent as she expected it would be. And she knew that was the moment she crossed the line. What she didn't know at the time was just how far across that line she would go.

†

Gwen shut her front door and locked it. She stood in the middle of her living room and looked around. Her favorite picture, the one of her whole family before things fell apart, perched on the oak cabinet in the corner. There were other photos tucked away in the drawer, photos that showed a young Gwen decked out in thick gold chains or leaning with her father against the tricked out convertible Camaro he loved so much. Those photos made her feel queasy, especially knowing now, as an adult, that the excessive spending by her father and so many of his friends was what cast the original suspicion on them.

She looked back to the photo on the cabinet that predated the drug days and wondered about PJ's family. She grew angrier. Why did she even care about someone who obviously didn't care enough to share about herself or her family? She wanted to throw something, but was too tired.

Gwen laughed suddenly at the absurdity of getting angry at PJ for not telling her all about her life. Gwen had enough secrets to fill a series of books, yet she was going to fault PJ for not telling all? Gwen justified her hurt by reminding herself that her secrets were all about the distant past. Well, all but the animal empath thing and helping her brother poach pythons....

She walked across the room and picked up the picture of her family. They were all smiling, but her mother's smile radiated the brightest. Gwen was convinced then, and now, that her mother was the most beautiful woman in the world. In this photo, they were on the dock in front of her dad's old crab boat. That was worlds away. Tears came. She slipped out of her shoes and shorts and curled up on the couch and cried herself to sleep.

"If I don't come back, hide in the boat's freezer, Gwenny. Hide in the freezer."

"Stay here with me mom, please, stay here!"

Gwen sat straight up on the couch. Her mom wasn't there. She hadn't been for a very long time.

Tears flowed down Gwen's face and she felt the ache deep inside her that was reserved for missing her mother. She missed her dad as well, but the hole left from her mom's death was unequivocal. It was probably exacerbated because of all the lies people told about her mom, about how no one believed Gwen when she awoke screaming with the knowledge of her mom's death almost three decades earlier.

Chapter Six

Gwen awoke abruptly from a dream. She heard her cell phone vibrating, but couldn't remember where she'd left it. She found it on the table near the door, still in the plastic baggy from her paddle home from work the afternoon before. She'd missed a call from Wyatt, but he called again before she even had the phone out of the baggy.

"Hey," she said.

"I need you to come to Dismal Key."

"Now?"

"Yep. Right now. And paddle hard, little sister."

Gwen put her shorts and fishing shirt back on. Her thoughts wandered to PJ as she slipped into her sandals. What was it about the woman that kept Gwen wanting to be around her when it was obvious that PJ was hiding something? She didn't need the drama of all that, but couldn't seem to stay away.

Her dream lingered in her mind. Even all these years later, the freezer still affected her. She would never forget how devastated she was as she hid there when she was so very young. She tried to shake off that feeling.

The burn in her arms and shoulders felt good as she paddled. She didn't like that Wyatt called her first thing in the morning, assuming that she'd drop everything, but it was also probably a good thing that she had something to distract her from thoughts of PJ.

She skirted the edge of the shell mound and mangrove island, mostly coasting and trying to hear where Wyatt might be. She couldn't see Robbie's boat and figured he had probably dropped Wyatt off and was lurking somewhere just out of sight. She landed at the clearing by the narrow path that led to the overgrown area around the old cistern.

The path had really grown up since the last time she was there. She slowly picked her way along the path while swatting at yellow flies. Shells crunched under her feet. Her clothes stuck to her skin. It was already a hot, humid day. The brush was so thick, all she saw was the slanted, rusting metal roof.

Gwen kept moving in the direction of the low roof, side-stepping several horseshoe crab shells. She jumped at sudden movement behind the cistern.

"It's about time," Wyatt said.

"It's not like this island is right next door to my house. Take what you can get, Wy."

He held out a pillowcase. She grabbed it by the twisted end and the heft surprised her. "Wow. This is a big one." A warmth spread from her fingers to her wrist.

"Yeah, sure is. Tell me what you think."

Gwen set the pillowcase on an area of sandy loam and opened the top of it. She spread out the opening and the large python inched out. Calm spread across Gwen. When

Anywhere, Everywhere

she held out her arm, the snake wrapped around it. Gwen had to use her other hand to support the rest of the weight. "Hey, sweetie," she whispered.

The python moved along Gwen's arm and across her shoulders.

"She's hungry," Gwen said. "Be sure to feed her as soon as you get her back to Robbie's."

"She's not going back to Robbie's."

"You already have a home lined up for her?"

"Yeah. Mine."

"Don't be reckless, Wyatt. That will be how you get caught."

"I'll be careful."

Gwen gently stroked along her side. "Why her?" she asked, but she already knew why. This was a special creature, a purely good creature.

"I've been waiting for the one that makes you look all soft and mushy. I can tell by your face that this one is special." He held out his hand then and the snake moved along the length of his arm. Wyatt smiled.

"Okay, sorry, but it's time to get back in the sack," Gwen said to the python. She looked up at Wyatt. "I'll meet you back at the marina."

†

As Piper approached the front door to the ship's store, she noticed the door to the bait freezer on the left wasn't down all the way. She gave it a little push until it engaged, just as she'd seen Gwen do many times.

There was a bit of an off smell inside. She couldn't quite put her finger on it, though.

A fifty-some year old woman was behind the counter, playing solitaire on the computer Piper had seen Gwen use to update the shrimp inventory. Piper cleared her throat when the woman didn't look up.

"Just a second," the woman said as she finished her game.

Piper looked around the store and noticed little things, like the trashcan overflowing, wet shoe prints crisscrossing the floor. It was those little things that showed how Gwen worked instead of playing card games on the computer.

"Can I help you?" the woman finally asked.

"Is Gwen working today?"

The woman looked at her then for the first time. She didn't even try to hide her assessment of Piper. "No, she's off."

"Well, hello," a booming male voice said from behind her.

Piper turned to find the store manager, Herb the perv, as she'd taken to calling him in her mind. She'd watched him enough with Gwen to know he was a real creep. "Hi," she said, trying to be nice, but not too nice.

"Can I help you with anything, darling?"

"No, thanks, I'm good."

"Well, I know you're good," he bellowed. "But can I help you?"

The way he looked at her made her want to throw up. Whereas the woman's assessment was just a catty thing, Herb's was downright gross.

Piper forced a smile and turned to leave the store. *Don't run*, she told herself. She kept her pace up until she was halfway to *Ruffled Feather*'s slip. She couldn't help looking over her shoulder several times as she went. She couldn't stand that Gwen had to work with that man.

She looked around the other boat slips, then unlocked the door and slipped into the safety of her rented boat. She locked the door behind her and moved the curtain open an inch to look out one more time. Glancing to the corner of the bedroom at where the shotgun leaned against the wall, she exhaled the breath she'd been holding.

Piper climbed down into the bilge where the freezer was. It had been making strange gurgle sounds before she'd ventured to the store. It still was. She pulled open the lid. All seemed still frozen. Deciding to indulge, she pulled out a chocolate-covered sea salt and caramel ice cream bar. Sticking it in her mouth, she bit down on the protruding stick as she climbed back up.

Piper sat at the small table in the main living area of *Ruffled Feathers* with her treat. She pulled the curtain to the side so she could watch the activities on the water. She was hoping to see Gwen, so when she caught sight of Gwen's yellow kayak, she smiled.

Gwen arced away from the docks. Piper had to shift in her seat to keep her gaze on her, then movement by the seawall caught her attention. It was Wyatt. Piper's heart raced as she watched Gwen paddle hard toward her brother. When she got closer she shifted her body and dragged her paddle. Just moments later she drifted gently up to the seawall.

Piper felt a little sick when Gwen handed a sack of something up to Wyatt. She had to ask herself how many times she would need to witness the handoff before she would admit that she knew exactly what they were up to.

She started to close the curtain when movement between the docks caught her attention. A small boat had its engine off and was drifting between the A- and B-docks. She couldn't make out the guy's face from under his ball cap. She had to admit that once they all dressed in fishing attire and went without shaving for a few days, the men all looked alike to her.

Piper jumped at the knock on her door. She pulled the curtain she'd been looking through shut before getting up and walking the few short steps to the door. She pulled that curtain to the side an inch and peeked out.

"Hi," she said as she opened the door.

"Hi, back," Gwen answered. "You busy?"

Piper laughed. "No."

"Would you like to go for a walk or something?"

For a moment she considered saying no. What if that man drifting between docks was looking for her? What if it was one of Gwen's drug dealer guys?

"You okay?" Gwen asked.

Piper felt immediately soothed by the question. "Yeah, I'm fine. Let me just grab my keys." She stopped and glanced toward the cabinet where she'd stored her Canon camera. She thought about bringing it with her, and then decided against it. She'd much rather keep her attention focused on Gwen.

Shouting from the direction of the fish cleaning station made Piper jump. Two guys were shoving each other.

"Arguing about whose is the biggest?" Piper asked. As soon as Gwen started laughing, Piper realized her double entendre.

"I really didn't mean it like that," Piper said as she followed Gwen along the seawall.

"Too bad, because that was funny as hell," Gwen said.

Piper laughed along with her. "I'm usually at my funniest when I don't mean to be."

Gwen shoulder bumped her.

Piper was glad to see that Gwen had obviously gotten past her anger at Piper for not telling her everything about her. "You and Wyatt must have a lot of fun together."

"We have our moments."

Thinking about Gwen's relationship with Wyatt, Piper couldn't help but miss Jeremy. The truth was, Jeremy was more of a brother to her than anything else. She wished he was there with her. He would approve of Gwen, of that much she was sure. And he would tease her unendingly about her attraction to the woman. She missed his teasing.

The shouting got louder and both women turned to see what was happening. Robbie had gone into the mix. Piper noticed Gwen's expression change as she watched. Piper had already figured out that Gwen was not Robbie's biggest fan. She wondered what the history between the cousins was, but knew not to ask or she'd be opening herself up to similar questions, as well.

Piper's attention went to a boat with two men turning in from the canal. The boat looked familiar, like maybe she'd been seeing it around a lot.

Gwen gave her a questioning look.

"Do you know them?" Piper asked.

"On the boat? I've seen them around. Why?"

Piper shrugged. She reminded herself that vigilance was one thing, paranoia something different. A fine line, but different nonetheless. Piper shrugged it off.

A group of a dozen birds made their way across the lawn in front of them. Most were white, but a few were brown and white. Their pink, downturned bills rapidly moved in and out of the lush grass.

"Those are interesting," Piper said. "Didn't we see some of the others when we were out in the kayaks?"

"We sure did." Gwen smiled. "They are white ibis. I call them sewing machine birds because of the way their bills move in and out of the grass so fast."

"If one is an ibis, is the plural ibi?"

Gwen's laugh burst forth in such a delightful way that Piper found herself floating along with it. "You are a funny woman, aren't you?"

Piper felt the heat rise on her cheeks and knew it wasn't from the sun.

"We used to jokingly call them Chokoloskee chickens when I was growing up. You can feed them and they get very used to people and, well, can end up in someone's kitchen if they aren't careful."

Piper's lip turned up at one corner. "You never ate them, did you?"

"No. Not me." Gwen smiled. "Here's a piece of useless trivia – they are the first birds to return to an area after a hurricane."

"I don't even want to think about hurricanes."

"Don't worry. I'll protect you." Gwen checked her watch, and then nodded her head to the side, indicating they should turn around. "I need to get going. Thanks for hanging out with me for a little while."

"Thanks for inviting me to. I, ah, I really do like it when you stop by."

The dazzling smile Gwen gave her sent her heart going into overdrive.

Piper watched through the curtain as Gwen strode away after walking Piper to *Ruffled Feathers*. She liked Gwen, and really hoped that Gwen wasn't into something too bad. She had to give her and Wyatt the benefit of the doubt. She wondered if there was anyone she could talk to. Who was she kidding? She was more afraid of the outside world as long as Bronson was out there than she'd ever be of Gwen or Wyatt, even if they *were* the new breed of drug smugglers.

Piper heard a wet, breathy sound through the opened window above the controls at the front of the boat. She leaned forward and pushed the curtain aside. When she looked down, she saw the snout of a manatee. She didn't think before she grabbed her camera and went out onto the dock. She was looking where she'd first saw the large mammal when she heard the blowing sound behind her. She whirled around just in time to get a picture of the creature's head. Her heart was pounding.

When it went back under the water, Piper kept her eyes opened but didn't see it again until its tail broke the surface several yards away. She'd read that manatees could hold their breath for three to five minutes, or up to twenty minutes when resting. It went back under and she scanned the area for the tell-tale sign of a swirl or flat spot on the surface of the water, an indicator of a manatee below, as Gwen had taught her. She started ticking off the facts she'd learned from Gwen. An average male was ten feet long and weighed between eight hundred and twelve hundred pounds, they could consume between ten and fifteen percent of their body weight in vegetation in a day and, except for short bursts, they generally traveled between three and five miles per hour....

The sound of voices from the efficiency apartment between her and the hotel made her jump. She was pretty sure it was just tourists talking, but realized then her mistake. She'd let the prospect of getting a good shot cloud her judgment. She hadn't even looked around when she stormed out onto the dock.

She went back inside and locked the door behind her. Then she shut and locked the window at the front of the boat. *What was I thinking?* she chastised herself, looking to the corner where the shotgun was for reassurance.

Chapter Seven

Gwen walked into the ship's store and cringed. The low-grade funky smell that always awaited her when she came back from her days off was there. She was pretty sure before she even looked, that the store would be a mess. She hated coming back to work and finding everything so dirty, but what could she do, not take days off? That wasn't an option.

On her days off, Jennifer and Stanley ran the store. Just like Herb did the opening shift, Jennifer opened on Herb's days off, and just like Gwen did the closing shift, Stanley closed. Sometimes who worked with whom would get shaken up, but it was usually to accommodate something Herb wanted a day off for.

Gwen wondered if her coworkers even had a clue as to where the mop and cleaners were kept. It sure didn't seem like it. She didn't even bother to talk to Herb about it because no concerns or suggestions from Gwen were ever taken seriously. Even when Herb worked with Jennifer, he didn't make her do the same amount of cleaning that he expected out of Gwen.

She walked behind the counter and right away saw the snuff spit trail going down the side of the desk into the trash can. She never could stomach how Herb didn't even bother to spit into something he could actually hit. She reached under the cabinet and grabbed a bottle of cleaner. She saturated the area and then left it until later.

After she'd straightened up around the register a bit, Herb came in. "Hi, sweetheart. Enjoy your time off?"

"Yes, I did." She couldn't resist letting him see her glance toward the mess dripping down the side of the desk. He ignored the look.

"I'm going out fishing with some of the guys. You know, it's important that I go out with the customers every now and then to bond."

"Yeah, I think you're right." She wouldn't let him know that it made her happy not to have him underfoot for a few hours.

He paused in front of one of the racks of hats and pulled one down. Then he yanked off the price tag and let it drop to the floor. He waved on his way out the door.

Gwen turned her attention back to the mess at the desk. She grabbed a pair of latex gloves she had stashed behind the bottle of bleach to keep Herb from taking them, and stretched them onto her hands. She gave the tracks of spit one last spritz of cleaner. The gunk came off pretty easily, but that didn't make it any less disgusting.

She saw movement in her peripheral vision and stood up. She froze when she saw Tracy Snyder standing beside the cash register.

"Hi, Gwen," Tracy said.

"What are you doing here?" She pulled off the latex gloves and tossed them into the trash can.

"Okay, I guess I deserve that."

"Does Wyatt know you're back?" Gwen asked, narrowing her eyes.

"I didn't come here to talk about Wyatt. I came here to tell you I'm sorry."

The last time Gwen saw Tracy, Tracy was fall-down stoned out of her mind, begging her for a few dollars. The next day, Gwen had noticed several of her favorite wood carvings were missing from her woodworking shop, along with some tools.

"I can accept your apology, but I can't welcome you back. And please stay the hell away from my brother – you've done more than your share of damage to him." Gwen turned and walked away from the register. She grabbed the broom and started sweeping the area between the coffee pot and the souvenirs. The next time she glanced toward the front of the store, Tracy had left.

Her hands started to shake. She had figured Tracy was long gone, either holed away somewhere far away or long dead, given her degree of drug abuse. She didn't want to think about that woman going anywhere near her brother. He'd just started being more like his old self the last couple of years.

"Don't fuck with my family," she whispered.

"Excuse me," a woman said as she approached Gwen.

Gwen hoped like hell the woman hadn't heard what she'd just whispered. "Hi, can I help you with something?"

The woman held up her camera. "I took a picture of a bird earlier and I can't figure out what it is. Can you look at it and tell me what you think?"

"Sure." Gwen reached for the camera once the woman had the picture pulled up on the little LCD screen. It only took a short glance at the mostly white bird with bluish smudges for Gwen to know what it was. "Yeah, that is an immature little blue heron." She walked behind the counter and pulled out a bird guide, flipping easily to the wading bird section. "See here?"

The woman leaned over the counter to get a better look. "Oh."

"They start out white, then turn blue. Yours is just at that in-between stage where it's changing." Gwen offered her the book.

"No, thanks. Now that I know, I can impress my boyfriend with my vast array of knowledge." She laughed, and then left the store with a big nod of gratitude to Gwen.

Gwen put away the broom and went outside. Tracy was nowhere around. She looked toward *Ruffled Feathers* and thought about PJ. That brought a smile to her face. She lifted the lid to the shrimp tank and was assaulted by the stench of dead shrimp.

She walked away from the shrimp tanks gripping the filters that she was pretty sure only got cleaned when she was working. She watched as Robbie lingered by the fish cleaning station. He lifted the lid to the scrap tank, looking to see what was being caught. Gwen cleared her throat as she approached.

"I don't know why you think you're so much better than me," Robbie said, out of the blue.

"I've never said that."

"You never had to. You lived in my parents' house all those years. The poor little orphan girl always got her way, too."

His front lip bulged. He was either running his tongue across the rough edge of his chipped tooth or was pushing the snuff around in his mouth. Repulsion set in. Robbie's chipped tooth had seemed so cool to her when she was young. She'd wished she had one like it before she'd even gotten all of her teeth. Then, as she grew up a bit and saw how creepy he was, the tooth had started to bother her. By the time she was seven and moving into his family's house there was something about him that had started to scare her.

Gwen turned her back to him and started taking apart the first filter.

"I think it sucks that your dad died in prison but what your mom did was unforgiveable."

Gwen clenched her teeth.

"At least with most of the other snitches, it was obvious why they left town. And a lot of them didn't go far, just to Naples or Fort Myers. Your mom was the worst kind, running off like that, abandoning her kid. No other mother I know abandoned their kids for someone else to raise. And she probably did take all that money like some folks think."

Gwen set the filter onto the scarred up cleaning table. She turned around and glared at Robbie. He stood there, looking smug, further infuriating her. She took the two steps to get to him and grabbed him by his shirt. She almost recoiled when she touched him and the hair on the back of her neck stood on end, but kept her grip on him long enough to throw him off the seawall into the brackish water.

She gathered her filters and started back to the ship's store. The filters would have to wait one more day. She glanced back once and saw a few tourists lingering about, one taking a picture as Robbie struggled to hoist himself onto the seawall.

As she approached the store, she saw Herb standing in the front window.

She put the dirty filters back into position in the tanks and went inside to wash her hands. Herb was gathering his things to leave for the day. "Behave, sweetheart," he said on his way outside.

"You didn't go fishing?"

"Change of plans." He scowled and Gwen wondered if maybe he hadn't been invited out onto the water after all.

She turned away from him and set about straightening up the counter a bit. He'd only been back a few minutes and had already messed it up.

Gwen looked up as her uncle approached the cash register. He glanced around, looking for what, she hadn't a clue.

"Hi, Uncle Derek, how are you?"

He narrowed his eyes at her, and then looked around again. "Mary Beth, you're playing with fire. You have to stay away from that Crews fellow."

"Uncle Derek – I'm –"

"What's with the uncle crap, Mary Beth?" He slammed his hand on the counter and Gwen jumped. "You spending time with Roy Crews is a dangerous thing. Stop that shit with him right now!"

Derek Hanes stormed out of the store. Gwen watched him. She wasn't surprised that he'd confused her with her mother, but didn't know who Roy Crews was or what he thought her mom was doing with him.

She tingled all over. Dread rose. She'd have to ask Wyatt if he knew anyone named Crews.

PJ came through the front door. "You look like you've just seen a ghost."

"It's nothing."

"You been busy?" PJ asked.

"Yeah, a little. But now I have to get the cooler organized." She smiled. "You want to go kayaking tomorrow afternoon? I get off at two tomorrow."

"Sounds great. I'll let you get back to it, then."

"See you tomorrow," Gwen said. She grabbed the coat she kept stashed under the counter for those times she had to spend any length of time in the cooler. She propped the door open, more so the customers would know where she was than for her to know where they were. Often she couldn't hear when people came in the store if her back was to the large glass doors.

She quickly organized the stock in a manner to make it easier for her to get the new stock behind the old when the beer truck came in the morning. As she worked, she felt the chill right down to her bones and knew she could never live anywhere but Florida.

As she left the cooler she pulled off the coat. She shut the heavy metal door and cocked her head when she heard Wyatt's voice. It was coming from back by the coffee maker.

"Did you get your lightbulbs taken care of?" Wyatt asked.

Gwen decided to straighten the shelves between her and her brother's voice. Then she heard Tracy's voice. "Yes, I did. Thanks."

Of course, Tracy had already seen Wyatt. Gwen intended to eavesdrop, but was distracted by the stuffed black panthers Herb insisted on having in the store. It was no wonder she couldn't teach the tourists the facts about the manatees and panthers, with people like Herb and Robbie always sabotaging it.

Gwen grabbed the broom and headed outside. A few minutes later, she looked up from sweeping the sidewalk just in time to see Captain Charlie, one of the fishing guides, throw his fish guts and scraps down to an alligator waiting in the water below. She charged to the cleaning station. "What are you doing?"

He looked at her and rolled his eyes. "Oh, don't you worry about us out here," he said, his voice condescending. "I got things under control."

Gwen pointed to the sign. "I know you can read. Throw your scraps in the receptacle, not the water." She glanced around at his customers, standing with their arms crossed, glaring at her as if they had a right to come into her world and screw it up. "A fed gator is a dead gator."

Herb came up behind her. "Relax, sweetheart. Why don't you go inside and mind the store. I'll talk to the captain."

She felt the heat on her face rising and the blood in her head pounding. She wanted to throw them all off the damned seawall, Herb first. She took a deep breath and looked at each customer very closely. Not a single one of

Anywhere, Everywhere

them better ever come in while she's working and expect anything extra out of her.

"Assholes," she muttered as she marched back to the store.

The bag of groceries on the counter – and lack of receipt with them – told Gwen what Herb was doing back at the store after he'd already left for the day. Apparently he'd decided he needed to do some shopping.

†

Tracy stopped short when Robbie stepped from behind the gas pump and onto the sidewalk, into her path.

"Well, well, well," Robbie sang. "What rock did you crawl out from under?"

"Just leave me alone," Tracy said from behind clenched teeth. She quickened her pace.

"Be nice, girl. You'll need me again one day and —"

She whirled around to face him. She had to face this head-on. "Never. Never again."

"You keep telling yourself that, princess." He spit his snuff spit onto the sidewalk, just inches from her feet. He smiled and his stained, chipped front tooth disgusted her.

"Screw you," she said as she turned and marched in the opposite direction.

"You wish," he called out to her.

She walked as fast as she could until she got to the door of the ship's store. She took a deep breath as she entered. *You got this*, she said to herself.

"Hello, can I help you with anything—" Gwen started her usual welcome but stopped short. "Oh, hi."

"Hi, Gwen. Do you have a minute to talk?"

She glanced around the store. "A minute," she said, her voice tight, clipped.

They stared at one another for a long moment. Gwen crossed her arms.

"I'm clean, Gwen. I know I could be good for Wyatt now that I'm sober. I love him."

Tracy saw the softening around Gwen's eyes. She and Wyatt shared so many expressions and mannerisms, right down to the crooked smile. Experience told Tracy that the softening features of Gwen's face meant that her attitude toward Tracy was softening as well.

"What step is this? Five? Six?" Gwen asked.

"Nine," Tracy whispered. "I am so sorry for everything I did to hurt you when I was using. I'm sorry I stole from you."

"You better not hurt Wyatt again," Gwen said.

"I won't. I promise. I am a different person now."

"You better be, because the person you used to be was worthless."

Tracy felt the stab, but knew it was true. "I know. I will prove to you this time that I am worth Wyatt's love."

Gwen nodded. "Okay." She looked around the store. "I have to get back to cleaning. I guess I'll be seeing you around."

Tracy smiled. "Yes, you will." She left the store feeling better than she had in a long time. She hadn't let Robbie get to her too badly, and she'd reached out to Gwen. The sense of accomplishment felt exhilarating.

As she walked to her new used truck, she thought about how that felt almost too easy. She turned to look at the store and reminded herself not to let doubt set in.

Her attention turned to an attractive woman walking from the A-dock toward the store. She had seen the woman talking to Gwen on a couple of occasions, from afar as she'd tried to get up the courage to talk to Gwen herself. Based on the body language she'd witnessed, there was definitely something simmering there.

She left the safety of her truck and approached the woman. The look on the woman's face made her regret her decision immediately. *Just say hi*, she told herself. She hoped that if she could get in good with Gwen's girlfriend then maybe she could help smooth Tracy's way back into Gwen's good graces.

"Hi," Tracy said. "I've noticed you with Gwen lately." She held out her hand and when the woman hesitated, Tracy quickly added, "I dated Wyatt for many years. I'm a family friend."

The woman took her hand and shook it. "I'm PJ."

"Gwen's new girlfriend?" she asked hopefully.

"I – ah –"

Tracy grimaced. "That was a little awkward, wasn't it? I'm so sorry. I can be a bit socially inept at times."

PJ smiled. "It's perfectly all right. And it's nice to meet you."

Tracy returned the smile. It felt good to make a new friend who wasn't in a twelve-step program with her, or forced to be around her at work.

†

Gwen paddled feverishly past her launch area at home. She needed some island time. Talking to Tracy had left Gwen in a bit of a panic. The woman was not good for Wyatt. She couldn't be trusted.

This was the type of day where, in the past, Gwen would have made a beeline to her wood shop. But she didn't spend time in the small structure by her house anymore. What was the point? Many of the tools she needed to carve were gone, and she couldn't afford to buy new ones. They'd disappeared at the same time the majority of her wood sculptures went missing. Which coincided with Tracy skipping town five years earlier.

What hurt Gwen the most, was that if Tracy had asked, she would have given her the wood figurines. But she didn't ask, she just took. The betrayal cut deep. Tracy had been one of the few people who made Gwen feel like she was important. Gwen had figured after Tracy sold the carvings and came down off her high, she'd come back. Maybe she would wait a week or so, but she always came back. But not that time. She didn't come back, not the next week, or month, or year. No, five years later she comes waltzing back.

She dug her paddle deeper into the dark water and tried to sweat out the anger she felt. How dare Tracy come back now? Wyatt was more like his old self than he had been in years and here she comes, charging back into his life.

"Damn her," she whispered.

She turned to the right to beach her kayak on the lagoon side of Camp Lulu, one of her favorite of the small islands. She pulled the kayak up onto the thin strip of sand, faced the gulf side of the island, and sat down beside the kayak. Steadying her breath, she watched as a group of pelicans dove head first into the gulf. She loved the rhythm of the waves and the diving birds. This was how the birds were supposed to act... their repetitive diving, natural, innate, doing what they were born to do before the influence of people turned them from excellent fishers to pesky beggars.

Movement from the direction of the island's only structure caught her attention. A pair of wet, scraggly raccoons came from under the old house and followed the edge of the island, glancing at her to make sure she kept her distance.

"I won't hurt you," she whispered.

She watched them until they were out of sight—camouflaged by, and under the cover of, the thick mangrove roots. She squeezed her eyes shut and heard her own five-year old voice...

"Mama, do you hear that?"

"Hear what, Gwenny?" her mother had asked.

"How scared this raccoon is." She'd cradled in her arms a very young raccoon, cocooned in a blanket, as her mother drove them to the veterinarian who lived a few blocks away.

Her mama slowly shook her head. "No, baby, I don't hear that."

"Maybe I don't really hear it, maybe I just know it?" Gwen asked.

"Yes, Gwenny, you just know it. And that's okay. I won't always know what you know, and you won't always

know what I do. And most of the world won't understand what either of us knows. Not the way we know things."

"I don't understand, Mama."

"I know, Gwenny, I know. One day you will. But for right now... right now you just listen...and feel...and just do the right thing."

"Okay, Mama, I will."

And all these years later, Gwen did understand most of it, and she did try to do the right thing.

She looked again at the small building. The wood-framed structure there on Camp Lulu was in relatively good shape. From what she understood, a caretaker looked after the place for the FWC, or whoever owned the property. There were stories about the man who had once lived here. A hermit, he wasn't poor or homeless, he just lived off grid. She'd heard once that if anything substantial was going on in the world that a buddy of his wanted him to know, he'd fly his helicopter over the island and drop a newspaper down to him. Like most stories in the islands, she wasn't sure how much of that was true.

She wondered if anyone used the small house anymore. At least it wasn't rotting away like so many of the old cultural landmarks. The last time she'd been to Dismal Key, famous for its own hermits, the path leading to the cistern was so overgrown, she could barely make it there to meet Wyatt. Gwen wondered when the cistern there was built and why she didn't know that piece of information.

Gwen was drawn to the islands where the history was more than just waves, mangroves, and people occasionally camping and fishing. Like the family cemetery and homestead ruins of Fakahatchee Island, the Calusa shell mound called Sandfly Island, where tomatoes had once been farmed, the long succession of hermits on Dismal, she liked the cultural landmarks.

She studied the steps leading up to the door of the structure in front of her. Gwen contemplated how one place could crumble with neglect while another —one even more exposed to the power of the gulf — stayed pretty stable. The structures were like the families of Everglades City after the big drug busts. Some families picked up where they left off after their men came home, while others, like the Martins, never fully recovered. Yes, Gwen had Wyatt, but without their mom and dad they were refugees of that drug crisis, not survivors like so many of the other families who'd come through the busts intact.

She wiped away a tear, reminding herself that growing sentimental would get her nowhere.

She'd gone to Fakahatchee Island with Wyatt and Tracy once. She'd been amazed that an island that was once just a Calusa shell mound was so rich in history, and that families who still lived in Everglades City had lived on the island at one time, farming it. The rain cistern seemed ingenious to young Gwen. Wyatt had told her about how the pilings, right off the island where he often fished for snook, once held up a fish house with two huge iceboxes. Now all it did was offer pelicans, cormorants, and terns a place to rest, and barnacles a place to cluster.

They had camped for one night on the high ground on the north end of the Fakahatchee Island, facing the bay. A man had also been camping there and they sat around a camp fire near the gumbo limbos. While Wyatt and Tracy were getting drunk and making out, the stranger told Gwen all about the trees that were once used to create the horses on merry-go-rounds since the wood didn't crack and was easy to carve. At the time Gwen wanted to carve her own merry-go-round horse out of gumbo limbo, but never got around to it.

"Now," the tanned, shirtless man had said. "Now they make them horses out of plastic." He'd given her a near-toothless grin. "You know what else they call them gumbo limbos?"

Engrossed, she'd shaken her head and waited for the answer so she could file it in her mind for another time.

"They call them tourist trees." He'd paused as he took a sip from his beer bottle. "Because they are all red and peeling like the tourists around here." He'd laughed heartily at his own joke, then stopped and cocked his head. "You looking at my eyeball?"

Gwen had grown concerned then because, yes, she had been looking at how the man's one eye drifted to the side. She lowered her head. Her mother had taught her better than that. "I'm sorry," she'd whispered.

"Well, hey, don't start pouting about it." When she looked up at him he said, "Look here." Then he raised his beer bottle and tapped the opening against his eyeball.

She jumped at the hard clanking sound.

The old man laughed. "Never seen a glass eye before, huh?"

Looking back, Gwen resented that Wyatt and Tracy had pretty much left her to fend for herself with this old, strange man. What if he hadn't been the harmless storyteller that he'd turned out to be?

Another time Wyatt and Tracy had taken her camping overnight on New Turkey Key. She was about twelve or thirteen years old. For some reason, Tracy had been trying to keep involved in Gwen's life. That particular night Wyatt and Tracy had been drinking again. Gwen had been content to watch the moon shining on the water until the clouds moved in. The storm and tide swamped the entire island and Gwen spent most of the night trying to keep the two passed out adults from drowning in their tent.

The morning after that, Wyatt bitched about the condition of their gear and about having to drive the boat hungover. Gwen still wasn't driving any motorboats since the episode years earlier when she'd been forced to drive her Uncle Derek's boat and accidentally hit and killed a manatee.

There were so many things to love about growing up in the everglades, even if there was also so much to hate, like the loss of her parents and the loss of trust that so many of the area's people had to endure. Didn't beauty often have its ugly underbelly?

The sun was casting an orange and gold glow onto the water on its way down. Gwen would be paddling in the dark as it was, and didn't want to get home too late. She mentally said goodnight to the handful of pelicans that were now bobbing on the water, took a deep lungful of the thick air off the water, and pulled on her gloves. She couldn't help feeling at peace, for that moment anyway, as she pushed her kayak off the beach into the backwater.

Chapter Eight

Gwen allowed her kayak to float into the edge of the mangroves. PJ followed. Just as they got close to the prop roots, PJ jumped, rocking her kayak.

"What is it?" Gwen asked.

PJ's eyes grew wide. "Spiders," she croaked. "Huge spiders."

Gwen gave a half stroke of the paddle to get closer. She laughed. "Those are crabs, not spiders."

"Oh," PJ said, seemingly composing herself. "Crabs."

"Come on, we can beach just on the other side of the island." She pointed out a slight indentation. "I used to be able to cut through here, but the mangroves have spread and closed up the gap between the two shell mounds."

PJ seemed to study the area but didn't speak.

Gwen led the way to the other side of the island, facing the gulf.

"Do all the islands have beaches?" PJ asked as she climbed out of her kayak and onto the rough sand.

"No. Some never did, some did but don't now, some might at a time in the future."

"Why do the islands change?"

Gwen pulled both kayaks farther up onto the island, and then stashed both paddles and gloves into hers. "Sometimes it's the wave action of the gulf, and sometimes it's the expansion of the mangroves on the oyster bars, like that area I pointed out."

"Mangroves," PJ said as she pointed. "That's the trees with the funny roots?"

"Yeah. Those are prop roots. A lot of the islands out here are nothing more than clumps of mangroves that have taken root on oyster bars." She was oversimplifying things and was okay with that.

"I met Wyatt's ex-girlfriend the other day."

"Oh? And how was that?" Gwen asked.

"She seems nice enough. Why did they break up?"

Gwen wanted to warn PJ about Tracy's manipulative ways, but felt that wasn't quite right since Tracy was clean now and probably would be harmless. "Tracy wasn't always as together as she seems to be right now. Just be cautious around her. I should probably leave it at that."

PJ just shrugged one shoulder. "Okay." She leaned to one side, obviously trying to see Gwen's back better.

Gwen was amused by PJ's unsubtle checking out of her tattoos. She was so happy that PJ wasn't as uptight as she had been the past couple of times she'd seen her. She was still acting a little nervous, just not as much so.

When she caught PJ staring at her shoulder again, Gwen turned and pulled away the strap of her tank top.

PJ reached toward her, and then stopped. "Can I touch it?"

Gwen nodded and PJ ran her fingers down the graceful curve of the neck of a great blue heron. Gwen watched as goose bumps rose on her skin.

"Beautiful," PJ whispered.

Gwen smiled, and then led PJ along the beach. She picked up a shell and studied it before she slipped it into her pocket. PJ did the same thing, several times.

PJ picked up a bright orange shell. "Wow, just look at the color."

"It's very nice."

PJ cocked her head. "You've only picked up one shell."

"Yes."

"Why is that?"

"That's all I need," Gwen answered. She took the scallop shell out of her pocket and ran her thumb nail across its ridges, then returned it to her pocket.

They continued farther down the beach and Gwen noticed that PJ had pulled all the shells from her pockets. She looked them over, compared them to one another, then put all but two back onto the beach. Gwen couldn't help but smile.

"Have you lived here your whole life?" PJ asked as they walked.

"Most of it."

"So, you weren't born here?"

"Yeah, I was. I went away to college in Gainesville—the University of Florida. I stayed up there for a while after graduation, but then came back." Gwen felt a twinge of guilt for not being forthcoming, but then again, PJ wasn't telling her much either. "Where did you go to college?" Gwen asked.

When PJ hesitated, Gwen grew discouraged. *This is it, please give me something.*

"I went to college in Virginia. I have a very versatile liberal arts degree." She shrugged as she spoke, as if apologizing. "What did you study?"

"Accounting."

"No way."

Gwen laughed. "What?"

"Seriously? Wow. I would have guessed something to do with wildlife or science."

Gwen wasn't surprised. All of the Everglades had expected that of her. She'd planned to be a wildlife vet when she was a child, but when the empathy was strong, being around all of the sick and hurt animals would have overwhelmed her. There was an injured possum that she'd tried to help when she was about ten or eleven years old. She hadn't been able to get him the help he needed and he had died in her arms. The feeling of fear, even after she'd tried to convey calm to him was so intense. Then when the life drained from his little body, she'd felt a draining of her energy that was downright terrifying.

PJ looked up as a group of pelicans flew by. "There are more pelicans out at the islands than in the marina, huh?"

"Yeah, and there's even more, farther out."

PJ nodded. "I've been reading online. This is an estuary, right?"

"That's right."

"It's beautiful out here. I love this whole area," PJ said.

"It is beautiful, but I'd also love to take you out into the swamp sometime. Waist high in clear, cool water. If you'll be around for a while."

Where did that come from? Gwen wondered. Gwen couldn't believe the sense of loss at the thought of PJ leaving. She wanted to show the woman everything.

PJ held her gaze.

Gwen leaned into her, kissed her, tasted her face, neck, and mouth. She knew what she was looking for and couldn't stop herself from doing it. She was trying to learn something from PJ's skin. She was trying to know something. What? Then she knew she was looking for a vibe to tell her that she could trust this woman.

Gwen desperately wanted to get a trust vibe from PJ. Just like with the pythons, like the baby raccoons, and countless other animals when she was a kid. But the vibe didn't come, so she decided that meant she couldn't trust this woman.

Oh, but she feels so good. Gwen kissed PJ's jawline.

But can she be trusted? Gwen's lips trailed down PJ's neck.

Was Gwen creating an excuse for herself? Was telling herself that no vibe meant no trust a way to convince herself she couldn't have intimacy and therefore, no broken heart?

You are pathetic, Gwen told herself. So what if the vibe didn't come? She had never truly read another human being. Even while knowing about her parents' deaths when no one else knew, it wasn't a true reading of either. Gwen grew angry with herself. She shouldn't try to learn what wasn't hers to know.

The wind started to pick up. PJ shuddered and Gwen wondered if maybe she wasn't the only one having trouble trusting.

Gwen looked up at the building gray clouds. "We really have to go," Gwen said.

"I know. I–" She took a deep breath. "Should I be sorry?"

"About?" Gwen whispered.

"Kissing you like that?"

Gwen couldn't explain the sudden urge to cry. "No," she said, hoping her voice sounded normal. She pulled PJ in once more and their mouths came together in a fiery kiss.

A gust of wind brought Gwen to her senses. The storm was getting closer much quicker than she had anticipated. She'd been so distracted by kissing PJ that things could actually turn dangerous. She silently berated herself as the rain started to fall.

"I could kiss you all day, but we need to get out of here before that storm really rolls in," Gwen said. She positioned both kayaks to launch, then stood with PJ to be sure she got hers moving okay. Once satisfied that PJ could paddle easily, Gwen jumped in her kayak and pushed off.

Thunder rumbled in the distance. *How could she have let the storm get that close?* Gwen chided herself. Lightning lit up the sky behind them.

Gwen felt the vibration of the boat rather than heard the noise of the engine as it rose above the sound of the rain and thunder. She was irritated to see Wyatt and Robbie pull up in Robbie's boat, but also a bit relieved.

"Let us tow you," Wyatt called out, holding up two ropes.

Gwen glanced at PJ. "It's not safe," Gwen answered.

"Safer than getting struck by lightning out here," Wyatt yelled. As if on cue, a bolt of lightning cracked open the sky.

Even though Gwen didn't want to share PJ with the guys, it was hard to refuse them. Her number one responsibility was keeping PJ safe. Reluctantly, she agreed and Wyatt threw her the ropes. She tied one to the front of each kayak, and then pulled PJ closer. Gwen stuck her paddle into the cockpit and instructed PJ to do the same. Then Gwen held onto the side of PJ's kayak. "Okay, but easy," she shouted.

They started out with a bit of a jolt, but then it evened out. Gwen wasn't thrilled though when she realized the men were towing them to Everglades City. She took a deep breath and tightened her hold on PJ's kayak.

When they made it to the dock and Wyatt tied them off, Gwen was at least glad that they headed toward Wyatt's and not Robbie's. All four were soaked when they reached Wyatt's small but tidy house.

Within minutes Wyatt had handed out towels and was asking who wanted a beer. After everyone had dried off as best they could, Wyatt fired up the grill on his lanai.

"Ever had permit, PJ?"

"Is that a fish?" When Wyatt nodded, she continued. "I don't think I've ever had it."

"Well, then today is your lucky day." He smirked. "Or maybe it's a luck*ier* day?" he asked as he looked at them both with his eyebrows arched.

"Wyatt," Gwen warned.

He laughed. "And little sister, today is your lucky day as well." He rubbed his hands together. "Because while Robbie boy was busy getting stoned on the boat today, I was respectfully catching this fine, *humane* dinner."

Gwen stared at him for several moments. The muscles around his eyes were relaxed, the perfect way to tell if he was being honest. She looked at Robbie and he quickly looked away from her. *Freak*, she thought.

"So, what do you say? You staying for dinner?" Wyatt asked.

Gwen smiled at PJ. "Unless you have other plans."

"Nope. No other plans," PJ said. "So, you're related to Robbie, how? Cousins, right?" she asked Gwen when the guys took up positions around the grill.

"We're first cousins. Robbie's father is my mom's brother. Well, *was* my mom's brother." She glanced outside and watched as Robbie downed a beer and reached for another. His shirt pocket showed the distinct, round outline of a snuff tin. She cringed. At least her brother gave that crap up long ago, thanks to Tracy telling him he wasn't allowed to come near her with that shit in his mouth.

Gwen would have to give Wyatt credit, the fish was wonderful. And the corn on the cob he'd thrown on the grill couldn't have been better. She smiled as she watched PJ wipe her mouth.

"That's the best meal I've had since I got here," PJ claimed.

"Thanks," Wyatt said. "Hey, Gwen, did I see you talking to Billy yesterday?"

"Yeah. He came by with some turkey salad."

Billy was one of the few people she would take turkey from. He'd hunted it legally and ethically – not always one and the same – and he chopped it and mixed it just right. If not put into a salad or stew, Gwen found the Osceola turkey of the Big Cypress to taste too strong for her.

"We need to get out there and get us a turkey this year. It sucks that the season is only a month long," Robbie whined. "Let's go out to Troy's camp next weekend and do some hunting."

"I ain't going out to Troy's camp this year. They just been busted for hunting over feed."

"So what? No one does it legal," Robbie challenged.

"That don't mean I want any part of it," Wyatt said. He turned away from Robbie and looked at PJ. "And you came here from where?" Wyatt asked.

"Wyatt," Gwen warned.

"From Virginia." PJ started to clean up the empty plates on the table. When she sat back down, she said to Wyatt, "It must have been pretty amazing growing up in a place that seems so full of adventure."

"It was pretty great. It was a better place before the government came in and told us how to fish, though," Wyatt said.

Gwen rolled her eyes. "Really? You're *going there* tonight?" she asked.

Some people from Everglades believed the National Park Service and FWC were conspiring to limit their fishing until they were all run out of town and the land and water was left for the rich people and environmentalists. Some thought the park service wasn't evil but was greatly misinformed and didn't know squat about what they were talking about. And if you asked someone with the park service, they would say that they had no choice but to step in because the area was being overfished, thanks to net fishing and other methods they worked to ban.

"Okay, sis, have it your way." He turned to PJ. "Some time when Gwen's not around I'll tell you stories about how the park service came in and wrecked so much for us."

"Oh, you want stories?" Gwen asked. "Let's talk about when you got caught stealing cigarettes from the store and Dad made you pay for them, then smoke every single one in the pack, one after the other until you started puking."

Wyatt laughed. "Yeah, but that's not nearly as funny as when John Booker dressed up as Skunk Ape and scared the shit out of Robbie."

"Hey, you gotta admit, it was realistic!" Robbie said.

"Oh, God, it looked like some cheesy ape costume right out of a B-movie," Gwen said.

"Well, if you had just dropped some 'shrooms you would have thought it was real, too." Robbie crossed his arms.

"What's Skunk Ape?" PJ asked.

"Gwen, you haven't taken her to the Skunk Ape Research Center yet? What kind of tour guide are you anyway?" Wyatt teased. He turned to PJ. "It's the Big Cypress Swamp equivalent of Big Foot."

"Except ours is real," Robbie said.

The polarizing, yet iconic, concept of Skunk Ape made Gwen smile. Whether you believed in the creature or not, the legend was a part of what made Big Cypress so unique.

Robbie finished his beer, and then smiled. "Hey, remember that one time we took Tracy out shark fishing? She'd never been before so we went way out into the gulf?" Robbie asked.

Gwen glanced toward Wyatt to see if he'd say anything about Tracy being back in the picture. His face was blank. Gwen had seen Robbie talking to Tracy outside the store the last time Tracy was at the marina. She could tell Tracy wasn't happy about seeing Robbie, and she'd practically run to the sanctuary of the store. She guessed no one wanted to acknowledge Tracy's return. She glanced at PJ and just got a little smile and wink from her, probably meant to tell Gwen she wasn't going to say anything about meeting Tracy.

"Remember?" Robbie prodded again.

Wyatt's face slowly softened and he laughed. "We fed Gwen biscuits and gravy for breakfast and got her on the boat without telling her where we were going."

Gwen shuddered. "I hated every one of you that day."

"I don't understand," PJ said into the laughter from Robbie and Wyatt.

"And now she won't go into the gulf with us anymore," Robbie added.

"Can't get her to do any decent chumming for us now," Wyatt said. "Now I gotta do it with dead shrimp."

"What's chumming?" PJ asked.

"Don't ask. And stay away from those two if you get at all sea sick," Gwen warned.

"Chumming is when you put the smelliest junk into the water to attract fish. Gwen puked into the water and all them biscuits and gravy lured in a whole bunch of sharks," Robbie explained.

"Eww," PJ said.

The look on PJ's face made Gwen laugh along with the guys.

PJ shrugged and smiled. "It's so pretty out here," she said as she glanced around the lanai.

"For now. Come summer it'll be too buggy to sit out here for too long," Wyatt said.

"Yep," Robbie chimed in.

"Gwen, do you ever drive a motor boat?" PJ asked.

"No. I prefer paddling. It's good exercise and better for the environment."

"Especially since you don't know what you're doing with a real boat," Robbie said.

Wyatt laughed. "Oh, and you do?" he asked Robbie.

"Hell, yeah, I do." He crossed his arms. "I can get us to any island out there from any other point without hitting a single oyster bar."

"Except Spider Island," Wyatt teased.

Robbie's eyes narrowed as he picked up his beer.

Wyatt directed his words to PJ. "I told him the other day that I wanted to go check out Spider and he got us all turned around. He was flustered and we ended up just going to Dismal Key instead."

"But we got us a real nice py–" He stopped short. "It worked out fine, didn't it."

What an idiot. Gwen looked at PJ, who didn't seem to have caught Robbie's almost-blab.

"We weren't talking about me and my boat. We were talking about Gwen," Robbie said, his voice whiny. "At least I never hit and killed a manatee."

"That you know of," Wyatt said.

"Tell your girlfriend the truth, Gwen," Robbie said. "Tell her how you don't drive a real boat because when you was little and my dad let you drive his boat, you thought you killed a manatee."

"Robbie," Wyatt warned.

"I was nine. I shouldn't have been allowed to drive Uncle Derek's boat," Gwen said. She paused. "What do you mean I *thought* I killed a manatee?"

Robbie turned to Wyatt. "You never told her we were just fucking with her?"

Wyatt sighed.

"I didn't kill a manatee?" Gwen asked.

"It was a log," Robbie said. He laughed. "This is funny shit."

Gwen stared at Wyatt.

"What?" he asked. "I liked having something to throw in your face when you got too high-and-mighty-earth-girl on me."

Gwen shook her head. She didn't even know where to begin with that one. "You are an ass, Wyatt."

Wyatt shrugged. "You been telling me that most of my life. Can't hurt my feelings now."

"Can I get anyone another beer?" PJ offered.

"Sure," Wyatt answered.

"Me, too," Robbie said before draining his existing can. He held it out to her.

Gwen grabbed the can from him and he glared at her. "Let me help you," she said to PJ. They went into the kitchen. Gwen noticed a change in PJ's demeanor.

"You okay?" PJ asked her.

"I'm fine. What's wrong with you, though?"

"Nothing," PJ answered, not making eye contact.

Gwen turned PJ to face her. "Something's bothering you."

"I guess I'm jealous. You have these family ties, these stories." She gestured around her. "This history."

"Everyone has history."

"I think I'm jealous of your relationship with your brother."

"Of that? He lied decades ago to me about killing something and I just now found out. Don't be jealous of that."

"But I bet he'd have your back with something important."

"Yes, probably. But it's not always easy between us. Besides, I'm sure you have someone in your life who could tell stories about you? Someone who could embarrass the hell out of you when you're trying to impress a woman. Like Wyatt does me?"

"No, not so much. Not right now, anyway." PJ cocked her head. "But let's get to the part about you trying to impress a woman."

Gwen smiled. "Let's not talk about that here."

She nodded. "Okay. But one day soon you'll have to tell me all about that."

"Do you want us to drop you back at *Ruffled Feathers* now?"

PJ looked through to where the guys were sitting. "No, maybe not yet." She followed Gwen back onto the lanai where the guys were arguing.

"I'm Everglades on both sides," Robbie said. "Y'all are only Everglades on your mom's side."

"Oh my God, you're arguing about who is more Everglades? That's the most ridiculous thing I've ever heard," Gwen said.

"Stay out of this, Gwen," Wyatt said. He turned back to Robbie. "You saying I ain't as Everglades as you are?" Wyatt asked.

"It's called a deepening of the gene pool, Robbie, don't knock it," Gwen chimed in again.

Robbie stared blankly, proving her point, Gwen thought.

As soon as they settled onto the couch, PJ asked, "So, this area has a bit of a darker history as well?"

"Pirates and rumrunners," Robbie said.

"Plume hunters and alligator poachers," Wyatt said, his eyes fixed on Gwen.

"And drug smugglers?" PJ asked.

All eyes went to PJ. Several moments later, Gwen spoke. "Yes, and drug smugglers." She leaned back in her seat and yawned. "Maybe we should get going."

"It's not like the drug smuggling thing is a big secret. Why won't anyone talk about it?" PJ asked.

"Because it dredges up a lot of pain from the past," Gwen answered.

She reflected on all the changed relationships. She wasn't the only one with trust issues after the big bust in the eighties. Friends had turned on friends in an attempt to sidestep jail time or get a more lenient sentence. Families were physically and emotionally torn apart.

"It's been almost thirty years," Robbie said. "And some people still ain't over it."

Gwen shrugged. "Sometimes there are just not enough years to make things right again."

"Or enough time to face the truth," Robbie added.

"Shut up, dude," Wyatt said.

"Why should I?" Robbie asked. "I'm so tired of not being able to talk about it. So your mom turned snitch and ran off with the money. Get over it."

Gwen could feel the color rising on her face and neck. She stood. "Now it's really time to go."

"And we won't even get into the part about her being so buddy-buddy with that dude who turned out to be DEA." Robbie stood, as if to face off with Gwen. "Your mom left you. So what?"

Gwen felt a stabbing pain in her gut. She fought to keep from bending in pain. She vividly remembered the moment she knew her mother was dead. No one believed her, but her seven year old self had no doubt.

Wyatt stood and stepped between Gwen and Robbie. "Okay, I think we can call it an evening, huh?"

PJ got up and took several steps toward the door.

Gwen was the first person outside and she immediately started loading the two kayaks into Wyatt's truck.

"Hey, little sister, let me help you with that."

"I don't need your damned help," Gwen said.

"You don't have to need it to take it."

Gwen stopped what she was doing. She stared at her brother. His words sounded just like something her mom would say. She stepped back and let Wyatt situate the kayaks.

Gwen sat between Wyatt and PJ in the pickup. No one spoke until they pulled up to drop off PJ. "Good night, PJ," Wyatt called to her as Gwen walked her down the dock to *Ruffled Feathers.*

"Sorry things got a little weird there at the end," Gwen said.

"If you ever want to talk about any of that, I'm a good listener."

Gwen couldn't imagine ever opening up to PJ about any of the past, especially not given the fact that PJ hardly shared anything with her. She just nodded.

PJ leaned forward and gave Gwen a peck on the cheek. "Good night."

"Good night." Gwen didn't let herself look back as she walked back to Wyatt's truck.

When Wyatt pulled up to Gwen's a few minutes later, he turned off the engine and faced her. "I thought for sure you'd punch Robbie for saying that about Mom."

She shrugged. "I gave it serious consideration."

"Why didn't you?"

"He's not worth it." She got out of the truck and stared at the kayaks. She'd forgotten to leave one with PJ. She grabbed them one at a time and placed them off to the side. She stepped in front of Wyatt's truck to keep him from leaving.

"What's up?" he asked as she came up to his opened window.

"Do you remember some guy named Crews back in the day?"

"Back in which day?"

"You know, nineteen eighty three."

"Crews? No, can't say that I do."

"I think he's the guy Robbie was referring to tonight."

"Where the hell is this coming from?" Wyatt asked.

"Uncle Derek mentioned him the other day. I was just wondering if you remember the name."

"Derek Hanes is in a whole other world these days, Gwenny. You know that."

Wyatt's use of her mom's name for her brought gooseflesh out on her arms.

"Yeah, I know. Good night. And thanks for rescuing us out there."

"Just another day in paradise," he said as he started to drive away.

Gwen went inside and collapsed on the sofa. She was exhausted. What had started out as a wonderful day spent with PJ – finally tasting the flesh on that soft part of her neck – turned into a trying day. She couldn't stop thinking about what Robbie had said. By itself it wouldn't be that big of a deal. But coupled with his father's ranting the other day when he mistook her for her mother…well.

She had the sudden urge to talk to someone who was an adult back in nineteen eighty three. She wanted to talk to someone who knew her parents. Aunt Linda would have been the best person to talk to. She'd been quite sharp right up to the point when she'd died of a heart attack, but she was no longer an option, and her uncle was obviously too far gone mentally. There was an old fishing guide that she seemed to remember lived in Everglades City when she was a kid. He often ran fishing tours from the marina. Maybe she could talk to him?

†

The front door opened and a man walked in. "You sell ball caps?" he asked Gwen.

"On your left," she answered with a smile.

"If it were a snake it would have bit me," he said. He grabbed a camouflage-patterned hat off the rack and started bending the bill. "This will do," he said as he studied the embroidered tarpon on the front of it.

As he set it on the countertop and pulled out his wallet, Gwen noted that his entire ensemble appeared to be brand new. There were still creases in his white fishing shirt, as well as his khaki shorts. He was very pale and she fought the urge to suggest sunscreen. He didn't look like the type of guy who appreciated people telling him what to do.

"Done much fishing?" she asked casually. The last thing they needed was a novice going out there and getting lost in the maze of mangrove islands that all looked alike.

"Huh? Oh, fishing. Not around here. What are they catching?"

"A lot of snapper. Some permit. A bunch of spotted sea trout." She rang up his purchase and took the twenty dollar bill he offered. She held out his change but he shook his head.

"Got a tip jar?"

She thanked him and stuck it in the need-a-penny dish. Undoubtedly, the change would be whittled down by the end of the day, especially if Herb noticed it.

"Have a great day," she said.

The man stepped out of the store and stood outside the window looking toward the A-dock. The hair stood up on the back of her neck. She watched him staring toward *Ruffled Feathers* for several moments before he walked away.

Gwen turned to watch from the other window as Captain Gary pulled his boat alongside the seawall. She waited until the two men on the boat climbed out and headed to the bathroom before starting in his direction. Gary was wearing long pants, a long-sleeved fishing shirt, a hat, and a buff around his neck.

"Hi, Captain Gary, you probably don't remember me, but –"

"You're the Martin girl," he said.

"Yes, I am. I used to see you around the crabbing boats when my dad was still – still around."

"I hated that happened to your father. Luke Martin was a good man. None of that was fair."

"I was wondering if I could ask you a few questions about that time, and well, especially about my mom."

Captain Gary rubbed his chin. "There isn't a lot I can tell you, that was a long time ago. And I didn't know your mom as well as I knew your dad."

"Anything you can think of would help," Gwen said.

"Your mom was quite a beauty. Your dad never did figure out how he got lucky enough for her to marry him. He loved her. Damn, he loved that woman."

Gwen watched him as he spoke. He adjusted the buff around his neck, then must have felt the need to explain it when he added, "Too many of the old timers are losing parts of themselves to skin cancer." He pulled on the long sleeves of his shirt. "I ain't taking no chances."

"I'm glad you're protecting yourself," Gwen said, more than a little anxious to get back to talking about her parents. "My dad was pretty handsome, too. I do remember my mom having the same reaction to him, like she couldn't believe how lucky she'd gotten, too."

His face distorted. "Seems to me there was some talk about – are you sure you want to hear this?"

"I'm sure. Please," Gwen said.

"There was some talk that she'd gotten involved with this fellow. What was his name? Roy, I think. Can't remember his last name. He wasn't in Everglades too long before they got, um, friendly."

"You mean Roy Crews, the agent they think she snitched to?" Gwen asked.

"Roy wasn't no agent, that much I do know. No, I mean the guy she fell for and ran off with."

"What?"

Gary reached into the back of the boat and pulled up a cooler. He grunted as he placed it on the concrete near the cleaning station. "We don't all like what we find out about our loved ones. You should probably leave this one be."

She stood up straighter. "I can handle the truth."

"I'm sure you can. But that's all I got for you on the subject. Sorry, but that was a long time ago and I've moved on with life." Gary leaned against the table, looking tired. "Some things are better left alone. I'm sorry about your mom

Anywhere, Everywhere

leaving and your dad getting killed. I really am." He turned and started to pull fish out of the cooler and onto the table.

"Thanks for your time," Gwen said before she walked back to the ship's store. Her mind was racing. One person thought Crews was law enforcement that her mother had snitched to, and another person thought he was her mother's lover. Gwen knew – just knew beyond a doubt – that neither was correct. Neither story made any sense as far as Gwen was concerned. There was something about the disappearance of her mother that they were missing.

She shook off the anxiety and started back toward the store. At least she didn't have too much longer before she could close the store and head home. Peter pulled his boat out of the water with his Ford F-350, and then honked to get her attention. She walked up to the passenger side window that he had rolled down.

"Can you unlock the gas for me while you're out here?" he asked.

"Sure." She pulled her keys off her belt loop and unlocked the padlock, then hooked the lock on one of the other belt loops. She started to walk away from the non-ethanol gas pump.

"Can't you pump it for me just this once?" Peter asked.

"You know that's against our policy." Even Herb stuck to that rule, but probably to keep from having to pump any gas himself. "I'm closing in thirty minutes so you might want to get gas before you hose off."

He gave her an agitated grunt and pulled his truck and trailer up to the pumps. A mockingbird landed on the side of his boat and he tried to scare it by fake-lunging toward it. It didn't budge, making Gwen smile.

"What you smiling about? That fucking bird waits all day for me so it can shit on my boat on purpose," Peter said.

"It can't shit on anything on purpose, it doesn't have a sphincter. Not one it can control like that, anyway," Gwen said.

"What? What in the hell are you talking about?"

She shook her head. "Never mind."

Gwen went inside and waited for Peter to bring in his credit card. When he did, he tossed it on the counter. She ignored him. He was rude the first day she met him, years ago, and continued to be rude every day since. She didn't let him get to her. She gave him his receipt and he left.

She started the closing out procedure, and then cringed when a truck pulled up. "Son of a bitch." She finished counting the drawer before she headed outside.

The gator wrestler visibly tensed when he saw her approaching. "I ain't got no choice, Gwen. It ain't up to me."

"I know it's not, Rick, but this is bullshit and you know it."

"The thing rushed at a man yesterday. It's got to go." Rick pulled out a large pole and a trip snare trap from his truck.

Gwen looked around at the crowd that had started to form near the boat ramp. She grew sick. A boulder of ice was growing in the pit of her stomach. She closed her eyes and concentrated. *Go away, go away*, she silently chanted her warning to every alligator around. They would just snatch the first big one they saw, and not even know if it was the right one. She grew aware of several in the vicinity. *Go away, go away.* Justice had been near the beginning of the canal when she'd come in that morning. She so wished she really could talk to the animals.

She noticed Justice going in the opposite direction, but several other alligators continued to hang around, and one was making a beeline for them. *Go away, please, just go away,* she begged. It continued toward them.

Rick got into position and Gwen started to walk away. She refused to watch this circus act. That was when she noticed Captain Charlie approaching in his boat with two fishermen. She stood by the gas tanks, just out of sight, watching Charlie instead of Rick catching the alligator.

The crowd had grown and moved closer around the ramp. Gwen closed her eyes as the ice boulder inside her grew. There was a collective gasp and a lot of splashing and Gwen didn't need to look to know exactly what was happening. She'd seen it enough.

When she opened her eyes the alligator was hogtied and its mouth duct taped shut. A few of the observers clapped. One asked where they would rerelease it. That was too much for Gwen.

She stepped out from behind the gas pump and approached the throng. Captain Charlie was standing beside the gator. Several people had taken out their cell phones and had been filming the entire episode. When Charlie nudged it with his foot and another visitor asked where they were taking it, Gwen couldn't hold back any longer.

"They aren't taking it anywhere to release it. The tying and duct taping is all just an act. The second they are out of sight, Rick here is going to put a bullet in its head."

"What?" someone asked.

"Yeah, I hope you all enjoyed the show because that is all this is. A show. A fed gator is a dead gator, and as far as I'm concerned, you," she pointed to Charlie. "You killed this gator by feeding it. And why? To look cool? To get a big tip from your loser customers?" She glared at them all as she raged.

She looked around and saw a curiosity about her on the faces of those standing around. They weren't outraged at what brought this gator to its impending death, no, they were too busy enjoying the show as she lost it. One person, a woman wearing a tailored fishing shirt and floppy hat, looked down at the ground when Gwen looked at her. She seemed to be the only person who even cared a sliver about what was happening.

"You should all be ashamed of yourselves," Gwen said before storming away.

†

Tracy knew without opening her eyes that Wyatt was watching her. She stayed very still for him for several moments before finally whispering. "What?"

She turned to face him straight-on as she stretched the length of the bed.

"Nothing," Wyatt answered.

She opened her eyes. "It's not *nothing*. Talk to me, Wy."

"I was just noticing how the lines around your eyes and mouth relax when you sleep."

Tracy chuckled. "So, you're studying my wrinkles?"

"I was remembering the woman I fell in love with."

Tracy could barely picture the woman she was then. She couldn't expect Wyatt to after all these years. "Ouch," she whispered.

"I don't mean it that way. I've always loved you, and even after everything that's gone on between us, I still love you." His voice softened with each word spoken.

Tracy could feel tears welling up. "I love you, too."

"Do you remember when we used to go camping in Big Cypress?"

She smiled. "Yes, I do."

"We should do that again. They charge and take reservations now, but we should still do it." He took her hand in his. "That sound good to you?"

"Yes." She smiled. "That sounds great." She wondered if he really wanted to do it or if he was just trying to get back to that place they were before she screwed everything up. Then she had to wonder if she was trying to get back to that place, as well. Yes, she was. Desperately.

"And we can go to the swamp buggy races this year, too."

"That would be great. I'd go anywhere and everywhere with you."

Wyatt chuckled. "I was thinking the other day about that pair of bright yellow Reeboks you liked so much."

"You used to say they were—"

"Butt ugly," Wyatt chimed in to finish her sentence for her. "You still have them?"

Tracy shook her head. She had hit rock bottom in Ft. Myers. She'd lost everything she owned and woke up in a ditch with only her panties and someone else's stained T-shirt on. Losing the little things like those shoes hurt much more than the jewelry she'd had to pawn for money to get high. "No," she whispered.

"We used to have some good times," Wyatt said.

"I remember taking Gwen out on *Ruffled Feathers* and you'd anchor and we would just hang out. We used to open both doors and jump out of them." She smiled. "And lying out on the deck, getting suntanned." She turned to Wyatt. "Your family had that boat for years, since it was built in nineteen sixty-six or sixty-seven. Why did you sell it?"

He stared at her for a long moment, and then took a deep breath. "Break my heart again, and you're dead to me. I swear."

"I know." She pulled the covers up to her shoulders as Wyatt shifted to bring their bodies in contact. "I know," she repeated. And she did. It scared her, but if she'd learned anything in rehab, it was that she couldn't let the fear of a normal life scare her into old ways.

Chapter Nine

Piper looked in all directions as she stepped out of the boat onto the dock. She was itching to get some photos taken. She promised herself she would stay on high alert, and if she felt uncomfortable or as if someone was watching her, she'd quit right away and go back inside.

She heard the shrill call of an osprey and followed the sound. She found it just as it began hovering far above the water. She focused on it and got a pretty decent shot, then it dove and she got an amazing series of it hitting the water and coming up with a fish. She hoped the water droplets dancing on the surface and dangling from the powerful talons came out clearly. What a rush!

A sound behind her made her turn. She didn't see anyone, but knew to stay vigilant. She turned back just as a bald eagle snatched the fish from the osprey in mid-air. By the time she got the camera pointed in the right direction, she only managed to get a distant, blurry picture of the backside of the retreating eagle.

"Damn it," she muttered. She brought the camera down from her eye, but in an instant reflex took over, and she caught the image of a mullet mid-jump. She was pretty sure the image would show the water trail left behind by the fish. She smiled. Okay, now she was hooked. Wildlife photography was so much more exciting than shooting weddings, and safer than sneaking around spying on men like Bronson.

She wondered what Jeremy had been up to lately. She missed him so much. She chuckled at the realization that he would not like this area that she had found herself growing more and more fond of.

The next movement that caught her attention came from the boat ramp. She used the telephoto lens to zoom in on Gwen as she stretched before getting into her kayak. The play of the sun on Gwen's glistening skin made Piper's heart beat faster.

She wondered where Gwen was off to. She'd hoped to hang out with her for a while, but it didn't look like that was happening. She stepped behind the boat, blocking Gwen's view of her as she paddled past. She knew Gwen turned to look as she skimmed by, she always did. That detail made Piper extremely happy.

Tracy pulled up in a small truck. "Hi, PJ."

Piper smiled. "Hi," she responded as she approached the vehicle.

"So, Wyatt mentioned the other day that you don't have a car. Do you need to go into town for anything? I'd be happy to run you there."

"Oh, I couldn't ask you to do that for me," Piper said.

"I'd be happy to. Really." She gestured with her head toward *Ruffled Feathers*. "Get what you need and we can run to the store."

Piper smiled. "Thanks. Let me just grab my wallet." She ducked inside the boat, put down the camera, and grabbed her wallet and keys. She double-checked that the lock had engaged before walking to Tracy's truck.

Tracy reached and removed a few things from the floorboard as Piper got into the passenger side. "Sorry," she muttered.

"No worries. My car at home has much more junk in it than this."

"You're from Virginia?"

Here come the questions. Piper was already regretting the decision to get in the truck with Tracy.

"Wyatt told me that. He also said not to ask you a bunch of questions if I spoke to you again." Tracy glanced at Piper, and then looked back to the road. "I hope I don't come off as being too much. I don't have a lot of friends around here, not since I've come back."

"No, you're fine," Piper said as she started to relax a bit. She was Wyatt's ex, and he obviously still talked to her, so she must be at least safe, right?

"There are a few things about me that you should know." Tracy smiled at her. "And I'm not telling you to make you feel like you should tell me stuff about you. I just think you should know these things right off." The expression on her face grew somber. "Oh, Gwen has probably already told you all about my misdeeds."

"No, Gwen hasn't told me anything about you."

Tracy stopped at a red light. She turned in her seat to look at Piper. "I am an addict. I'm in recovery, fresh out of rehab, but I am an addict."

Piper felt uncomfortable for just a moment, then grateful. At least Tracy was being honest. "Okay."

"I was not a good person when I was using." The light turned green and she moved through the intersection. "But I'm also no longer that person."

Piper nodded.

"Where to?" Tracy asked.

"I do need to grab some groceries, but first I would absolutely love a burger. Not some gourmet thing, just a good, old-fashioned fast food burger," Piper said.

"Now, that is a plan," Tracy said.

Piper smiled when Tracy pulled into McDonald's. She couldn't help but think of how Jeremy would lecture her about her semi-occasional visits to fast food joints. He'd tell her she was addicted to the salt-laden food and it would kill her. Little did they know until recently that it would more likely be her photography that would be her demise, not her diet.

They sat down in a booth with their burgers. Piper wasted no time tearing into her double cheeseburger. She caught Tracy watching her. "What?" she asked with a knowing laugh.

"I think your enthusiasm is a nice change. Are you getting tired of living out in the middle of nowhere?" Tracy asked.

"No, not tired of it. I do miss being able to eat at a sushi restaurant, or Greek, or Mexican, or anything else within five minutes if I get the whim to. But, there's an upside to living out there, too."

"Is the upside named Gwen?" Tracy asked.

Piper couldn't hold back a huge smile. "Yeah, you could say that."

"The Martins are good people."

Piper nodded. She was extremely curious about the Martins and Tracy and the relationship between them all. "Tell me about you and Wyatt."

Tracy took a small bite of her burger and slowly chewed it. Piper could tell she was measuring her words. After several moments, Tracy took a sip of her soda. "Things with Wyatt and me are complicated."

"How did you meet?" Piper figured that was one of those topics that got people talking and led to other things being said.

"I was a senior in high school, he showed up at a football game there with some buddies of his." She smiled and Piper waited for several moments, Tracy obviously deep in thought about those days, until she continued. "He was nineteen. I was seventeen. I was smitten right away. But, things didn't work out and we lost touch for a while."

Piper sipped soda through her straw. "Then?"

"Then the next time we met up, we didn't let life get between us for several years. My problem with prescription pain pills ended up being the end of us. We were off and on because of my drug issues for years and years." She gave an exaggerated shrug. "And here we are. Enough about me and Wyatt. Tell me about you and Gwen."

"Well," Piper said. "There isn't really a lot to tell. We've been spending time together, that's all."

"Is that what you call it these days? *Spending time together?*"

It took a minute for Piper to realize what Tracy was asking. "Oh, ah, no, we haven't done *that* yet."

Tracy laughed. "Why is your face so red? And what in the hell are you two waiting for?"

Piper couldn't help but laugh along. "I don't know. She's not the easiest person to get close to."

Tracy grew serious. "She doesn't open up to a lot of people and she doesn't trust easily."

"Because of her family's history in Everglades City?" Piper asked.

"Yeah, mostly."

Tracy looked away and Piper was sure there was something else, as well, maybe something between Tracy and Gwen that turned into a trust issue?

"I heard a few things one night with Gwen, Wyatt, and Robbie, but it just left me more confused than ever. Maybe you could tell me about their family?" Piper asked.

Tracy gathered up her trash and put it in the corner of her tray. "I don't think I should tell you things about the Martins. Don't you think you should be talking to Gwen about her family?"

Piper nodded. Of course she should. "How about the town? Tell me about Everglades City?"

"What do you want to know?"

"Is it true that in one night most of the adult male population was arrested?" Piper asked.

"That's a bit of an exaggeration," Tracy answered. "That night everyone talks about there were only about twelve guys arrested in Everglades. But another bunch were arrested at the same time in Goodland and Naples."

"Why does Everglades City get the bad rap for smuggling when they weren't the only ones?" Piper asked.

"That's a good question. Wyatt would say that is because people always think worse of the working folks." Tracy shrugged. "It might not have been a lot of people that night, but there were other busts, and other people who got arrested after their so called friends ratted them out."

"Or their families?" Piper ventured.

Tracy nodded. "So many of the fishing boats were confiscated, that it crippled the fishing and crab businesses. The effect was just so concentrated in Everglades, compared to the other areas."

"Wow," Piper said.

"Overall, the busts altogether put about two hundred people in jail in southwest Florida. For everything from hauling pot, to tax evasion, and contempt of court."

"Didn't I read where some judge was involved but never went to jail?"

"I don't think that judge was ever caught. He got the hell out of dodge and never looked back."

"Doesn't seem fair," Piper said.

"In the end, people like the judge escaped justice, but not Luke Martin or the rest of the regular folks. Once the money was stripped from them, they didn't have power like the judge did. Wyatt was left with *Ruffled Feathers*, the Hanes had their house but not much else, and Gwen...well, Gwen had nothing." She looked away with those last words.

"Why did so many people smuggle drugs? They had to know they might get caught."

"Wyatt's Uncle Derek used to say it was all a matter of too much temptation, especially with the young guys in their twenties," Tracy said. "And so many of them thought they were so far off anyone's radar that they'd never get caught. Until the folks started spending some of that massive amount of cash. That's when they got noticed."

"You're not from Everglades City?" Piper asked.

"No," Tracy answered. "I'm born and bred Naples."

"I've always been curious about towns with such deep history. How many generations does a family have to live in Everglades before they're considered from there?" Piper asked.

"It's how you act while you're there, not how long you're there that matters. If you don't go in expecting them to all change to fit you, then you'll belong. But you got to fit in, you don't get to try to change them." Tracy fidgeted with her paper cup.

"Are the Martins from Everglades City?" Piper asked.

"Wyatt and Gwen's mom was from there. Their father moved there in his early twenties."

"Was he considered from there?" She vaguely recalled Wyatt and Robbie arguing about one being more Everglades than the other that night they'd all had dinner.

"Oh, yeah. Everything I've ever heard about him was that he embraced Everglades immediately, and them him. It was love at first sight for him with both the town and with Mary Beth," Tracy said. She gestured toward Piper's tray. "Done?"

"Yes. We should probably get going," Piper said. "Thanks for telling me some of the history there."

"You are quite welcome. Groceries?" Tracy asked.

Piper nodded. "You sure you don't mind carting me around?"

"It's my pleasure," Tracy said in a voice that made Piper believe her.

It pleased Piper to have a friend.

It was a short drive from there to Publix. Piper had enjoyed shopping there with Gwen. She'd learned so much about the woman while going up and down the aisles, including the fact that Gwen would not think the burger Piper had just eaten was ethical eating. Would she question every food decision now that Gwen put that thought into her head? Well, she reminded herself, it didn't keep her from wolfing it down a few minutes earlier.

Piper and Tracy shared a cart, each just keeping their groceries to one side. Piper was half way down the wine aisle before worry creeped up. She looked at Tracy and couldn't read her expression.

"Should I not get a bottle of wine? I don't want to make you uncomfortable with it since you're —"

"It's fine. I'm fine. Thanks for worrying, but I won't shove you to the ground outside and grab the bottle and run. I promise." Tracy gave her big smile. "Seriously, thanks for asking."

Piper returned the smile.

A few minutes later, Piper watched Tracy study a package of Oreo cookies. "My dad and I would share these things every afternoon when he came home from work. Until I was about thirteen or fourteen. Then I just started disappointing him every time I turned around."

She put the cookies back on the shelf. "And he disappointed me when he started pulling away from me instead of trying harder with me when I started using. Anyone ever disappoint you? Have you ever disappointed anyone?"

"Not anything big like that. For me, my disappointment in others has always been an accumulation of little disappointments. But oh, was my mom disappointed in me when I divorced Jeremy. She cried for weeks."

"You were married to a man?" Tracy asked.

"Yes. And no, Gwen doesn't know."

Tracy laughed and threw her hands up. "Trust me, I will never judge you."

"The first disappointment I can remember was when my family first moved to Virginia. My parents had talked for months about moving to a ranch house. I had all these fantasies of what I would do on that rambling acreage. I hoped maybe my dad would let me have a horse."

She grew anxious. Her dad had driven their sedan down from Pennsylvania and he'd announced that they were almost there as they drove through a cookie-cutter neighborhood. How could they be almost there when they were surrounded by all those flat, brick houses?

"When my dad pulled into the driveway of an orange brick house and announced 'We're here!' I sat in the back seat and tried to wrap my brain around how that *thing* could be our ranch house. Where were the rolling pastures? The room for a barn and horses?" Piper signed in defeat.

"The whole time they meant a ranch style house," Tracy added.

"Yep. Took me years of confusion to figure that out."

"No wonder you were disappointed."

The rest of the day was in a slow-motion, stunned silence as her mom excitedly showed her the house and the half-acre yard that wasn't near the vast expanse of land her young imagination dreamed it would be.

They paused in front of the ice cream case. "You know what always makes me feel better?" Tracy asked. "Gelato."

"Yes. I think I will take some salted caramel," Piper said.

"Nice choice, but I'm having butter pecan." They each put their selections in the cart and headed toward the cash registers.

Piper couldn't believe how much she had told Tracy, but she didn't mind. Tracy was easy to talk to and well, safe. She didn't really mind her new friend thinking she was a dork, but didn't want Gwen to think that. Not too early in the relationship, anyway. She smiled at the thought of a relationship with Gwen.

†

Gwen chuckled at the sight of Wyatt half-hanging from the mangrove with one hand, a propagule poking into the side of his face, and his monkey feet gripping the roots for balance. Her amusement ended when she noticed the bulky pillowcase grasped in his left hand. She coasted up beside him.

"You're late. Where have you been?" Wyatt barked

"Thanks for calling me out here against the tide. And you're welcome."

Wyatt let go of the branch and grabbed the front of the kayak to pull her closer. He almost tipped her trying to catch his balance.

"What do you have?" she asked.

"Burmese." He tried to hand the pillowcase off to her. "Quick, FWC is right on the other side of this island."

When Gwen still didn't take it, Wyatt shoved it between her knees, into the cockpit of the kayak. "Take it and get the hell out of here." He gave the kayak a shove. "Go, go, go."

She resisted the urge to smack him with her paddle, and instead dipped it into the dark water. The tannin from the mangroves gave it a dark reddish-brown color that concerned people new to the islands, but the locals weren't at all bothered that the water wasn't the crystal-blue of the Florida Keys.

When she heard the low rumble of a boat, she pushed the pillowcase down around her feet and started paddling.

"Hey, Gwen, where's Wyatt hiding?" the Fish and Wildlife officer asked.

Gwen gave an exaggerated shrug. "If he's hiding, he's hiding from me, too," she teased. She racked her brain trying to remember what this officer's name was. It didn't come to her.

"I hear you. What are we going to do with that brother of yours?"

"Oh, I have some suggestions," she shot back. At the sound of his laughter, she turned away and paddled harder.

She felt the weight of the snake in the cotton sack shift against her ankle. She couldn't get a read on it like that, but maybe that was for the best. She concentrated on

Anywhere, Everywhere

paddling toward the canal that would take her to the marina. She moved her leg when the shifting against her feet grew.

She knew a second before she felt the snake sans cotton sack against her skin what had happened. She shuddered. When its tongue tickled the soft flesh on the inside of her ankle, she forced herself to stay calm.

She glanced around to see if there was a good landing area on any of the small mangrove islands nearby. Nothing looked workable. She kept paddling, hoping the snake would stay around her feet. As soon as she thought it, the snake slid up and wrapped around her calf.

Please, don't bite me, she pleaded silently.

FWC officer, Duane Shivers, hailed her then pulled his boat up just close enough so Gwen could hear him, but not so close that his wake would rock her too much. He killed his engine and waved at her to come over. She paddled gently, hoping not to spook the loose snake any more than it already was. "Hey, Duane, what's up?"

"I was just talking to my fellow officers and we think it's strange that all of a sudden you're seen more and more with your brother out here. Or worse, out here at the same time, but not actually with him."

"I know," she tried to joke. She shivered as the snake tightened around her leg before inching up her thigh. "The company I keep, huh?"

"We know Wyatt's up to something. And I sure hope you aren't a part of anything illegal with him, Gwen."

Gwen shrugged. "I'm just out getting some exercise and enjoying a beautiful day."

"You know I like you, Gwen."

Too much, perhaps? she wondered.

"So, this is your one and only warning. If you are up to something with your brother, you will get caught. After right now, I will be searching every inch of your kayak if I see you out here with Wyatt, and then paddling off without him. Understand?"

She shivered as the snake moved higher. "Understand. I promise you that you will not find me involved with anything illegal with my brother." *From the moment I hand this snake off to him.*

"Good. Have a great day." He started his engine but waited until she paddled away before moving.

"Son of a bitch," she whispered. Now, there was not a doubt in her mind that this was the absolute last snake she helped Wyatt with.

The snake wrapped tighter around her leg and she sensed its fear. She took a slow, deep breath, trying to send out a calming vibe. She beat down her thought of killing Wyatt for getting sloppy with the way he tied off the pillowcase. No negative energy, she reminded herself.

She looked down and could make out its distinctive, giraffe-like pattern as it wound higher up her leg. The fear she felt from it lessened and she paddled carefully, trying not to make any erratic movements. Breathe, she reminded herself. Breathe and paddle.

She relaxed a little as the end of the C-dock came into view. The snake constricted tighter around her thigh. As she saw Wyatt back his truck into the parking space closest to the edge of the dock she felt a little better. Until she glanced down and saw the python's head just a little too close to her crotch.

She reached her hand down between her legs and it slid up her arm.

"Hi, there," she whispered. The gentle vibe she got from it made her relax.

She used her foot to inch the empty pillowcase upward. "Sorry, but it'll only be for a little while." She slipped the case's opening over the snake's head. The python went right in. "I know, you feel pretty safe in there. It'll be all right."

A few more strokes of her paddle, then she coasted in to the side of the dock. She drew up beside Wyatt. She reached up to hand the bulky pillowcase to him. "A real sweet one."

He gave the untied pillowcase a questioning look.

"You can tie it off. And I hope you do better this time than you did the last. And this is the last one, Wyatt. I swear." She was about to paddle off when she saw Captain Gary watching her. She followed the seawall toward him. "Hello, Captain."

"Hello, Gwen. I wanted to give you this." He held out a slip of paper.

"What's this?" She took it from him.

"It's the name of a retired FBI agent I knew back in the eighties. I told him you might be calling. He's local."

"He knows something about my mom?"

Gary shrugged. "Don't know for sure if he does. But I do know that he's a good guy and you can trust him. If there is anything more to the story and he knows it, he'll tell you."

She slipped the scrap of paper into her shirt pocket after glancing at the name. *Dale Townsend.* "Thank you. I really do appreciate it."

He tipped his hat to her. "Well, we locals got to stick together, now, don't we?"

"Yes, sir, we do." She turned away and Duane Shivers waved her to the side of the dock he was tied off to. She paddled to him, glad she didn't have a snake with her now.

"Sorry, Gwen, but I meant to talk to you about something else when I saw you earlier."

"What's up?" she asked, trying to sound casual.

"It's about Derek Hanes."

"Oh."

"Your uncle's been messing with Fred Dalton's crab traps out on the water."

"I don't think I know Fred Dalton."

"Apparently he throws his traps where Derek used to. He's complaining that Derek's pulling them. No one has seen him take anything, but if they do, there will be hell to pay. And in the meantime, Dalton's getting pissed that he's even touching them."

It was no small thing if someone messed with your traps. Stone crabbers often had their favorite places for throwing traps, and folks showed a lot of the old-timers respect by not throwing their own in those guys' locations. Guys like Derek Hanes had been crabbing the same places for decades, or sometimes generations.

She'd heard a story around town once about a man who had been caught taking from someone's traps. The traps' owner got some buddies of his together and paid the guy a visit at home. Apparently, they'd stripped him down to his boxers and tied him to a chair in the middle of the room. Then they went through his house and picked out some items they liked, and said they planned to keep. "See," the owner of the traps allegedly told him. "Now you know how I felt when I learned you done stole from my traps." In the end they didn't take anything from the guy, but they sure did teach him a lesson.

"Gwen?" Duane prompted her.

Gwen chose her words carefully. "I'm sure Derek doesn't mean any harm. It's probably just an old habit coming back to him."

"You mean the old man doesn't remember they aren't his traps anymore? It isn't a big secret that he has some, how should I say this?"

"Some cognitive issues?" Gwen helped him out.

"Yes, some cognitive issues. Gwen, can you talk to him? Fred is mad enough that he's touching them, if he even thinks the old man is removing crabs he's going to go nuts on him."

Gwen shrugged. "I can try to talk to him but don't know if it will do any good."

"I appreciate that. Sorry to bother you with this but I didn't think it'd do any good to talk to Robbie. That man is worthless."

Gwen didn't disagree with his assessment of her cousin. "I'll try." She decided she would wait until Derek mistook her again for Mary Beth since he listened more to his sister than he ever did anyone else.

Chapter Ten

Piper watched as Gwen glanced around the inside of *Ruffled Feathers*. Gwen nodded toward the camera on the seat by the small table. "Been taking photos?"

"Yeah."

"I'd love to see them sometime."

Piper knew she had to give Gwen something. "Okay. I just put a few on a flash drive if you'd like to see them."

"Show me now?"

"Sure." There was something else much more intimate that she would rather show her, but that would have to wait. She wasn't going to let this chance to make Gwen happy slip away. She pulled out her laptop from the cabinet behind her and powered it on. She put the drive into the USB port and waited a few seconds. Once she had them up, she let Gwen slide through the photos. She was glad then that she had put the photos she'd taken of Gwen onto a different flash drive. She'd hate for Gwen to think she was a stalker.

Gwen stared at a shot of an osprey with a large snook in its talons. "Wow, you're really good."

"Thanks."

"You this good with wedding photos?"

It felt like a test to Piper, but she just smiled. "Yes, I am."

Gwen took the laptop from her and set it in the chair opposite the one with the camera perched on it.

"I'm glad you're here," Piper said as she took a step toward her.

"I'm glad I'm here, too," Gwen said. "Do you know how long you will be here?"

"I might be another week... or a month... or, who knows?" Piper said. "But I would love to spend that week, or month, or who knows, being with you."

"I know nothing about you," Gwen said.

"You know I'm afraid of spiders. And that I know nothing about birds except what you've taught me. And that...." She placed Gwen's hand over her heart. "And that you make my heart pound every time you get near me."

Gwen smiled. "Yeah, there is that." She leaned into Piper and kissed her.

"And you know that when you accidentally brush against my breast." She brought Gwen's hand to her left breast. "That my nipple hardens."

Gwen gasped. "And there is that. But I don't know what happens when I place my hand here." Gwen cupped her hand between Piper's legs.

Piper shifted until Gwen could slide her hand down the front of her shorts.

A bolt of pleasure hit Gwen between her legs as her fingers dipped into PJ's wetness. "Oh, and that. Yes, there is that."

Goosebumps formed on Piper's arms when Gwen pulled her close and kissed her.

"I want to get to know you," Gwen whispered. "I want to know every inch of you."

Piper took Gwen's hand and placed it back on her left breast. "Want to start here?"

"Not just physically," Gwen said.

"Oh, but isn't this a nice place to start?"

Gwen slipped her hand under Piper's tank top and rolled her nipple between her thumb and forefinger. "A very nice place."

Piper moaned when Gwen's other hand joined the one already under her shirt and she kneaded both nipples at once. "That feels wonderful."

Gwen kissed her as she squeezed both nipples.

"Yes, harder," Piper begged.

Gwen's mouth made its way down Piper's neck.

Piper ran her hands along Gwen's sides. "You feel so good."

Gwen groaned, and then removed her hands from under Piper's shirt. She worked the button of Piper's shorts undone. "Let's get you out of these."

Piper dutifully slipped them off, then her panties. Her breath caught when Gwen turned her around and embraced her from behind. She tilted her head back as Gwen ran her tongue along her neck and caressed her breasts.

As Gwen continued to work her breasts, Piper felt a little weak and leaned forward to rest her hands on the small table by the window. Gwen grasped her by the hips and pulled her ass closer. "You are so damned hot," she whispered as she ran her hand between Piper's legs.

Anywhere, Everywhere

Piper could only groan in response.

"You like it like this, from behind?" Gwen asked, her voice raspy.

"Yes, yes, you feel so good. Please. Please, go inside me."

"Ah, you do like that, huh?"

"Yes, yes, please."

Gwen used the fingers of one hand to spread her labia, then stroked against her wetness with the other. She slid one finger in, then another, and another. She rocked against Piper as she filled her from behind.

Piper felt the tide of orgasm building as Gwen worked her fingers in and out of her. Each time Gwen filled her she slid forward a little, taking the table with her, causing the curtain on the round window to shift back and forth.

"I love the way my fingers feel inside you. You are so wet, so very wet." Gwen leaned lower as she spoke, adding another angle to the pressure Piper felt against her clit.

Piper's eyes were half-closed as she tensed, preparing for her orgasm. Gwen filled her and she opened her eyes a little wider, just as the curtain shifted and she saw a man in a boat, checking out *Ruffled Feathers*. It only half registered before her attention returned to Gwen's fingers pumping in and out of her and the world started to spin with her climax.

"Oh. My. God," Piper managed to croak.

Gwen removed her hands and helped Piper to stand. "You okay?"

"Never better," Piper whispered. She wrapped her arms around Gwen. She knew there was something she meant to say to her, but before it registered, she was undressing Gwen.

"Take me to the bed?" Gwen asked.

Piper nodded, but couldn't speak as the heat rose throughout her entire body. She let Gwen lead her into the bedroom. Without a word, Piper cleared the stacks of clothing off the bed with a swipe of her arm, letting them land haphazardly onto the floor.

Gwen didn't wait for her to turn down the comforter before pulling Piper onto the bed with her. "I need your hands on me right now," she said into Piper's neck. "And your mouth."

"Yes, yes," Piper whispered. She clawed at Gwen's shorts and pulled them down her legs, dragging her panties along with them. She settled the weight of her body over Gwen and pressed into her. Gwen's moan sent ripples of pleasure through her. She pressed harder and ground her wetness against Gwen's clit.

"You feel so good."

Piper slipped her hand between them and found Gwen's clit with her thumb. She rubbed against the hardened clit, spreading her wetness.

"Go down on me," Gwen gasped. "Please."

Piper let her mouth trail down Gwen's body until she reached her wetness. She plunged her tongue into Gwen and the ensuing moan threatened to make Piper come again.

She lapped at Gwen until she grasped her hair and held tight while her body convulsed in orgasm. "Yes, come, come," she chanted into Gwen's bucking body.

Later, they lay on their sides, front to front. Piper squeezed Gwen tighter.

"You are wonderful," Gwen whispered.

Piper gave Gwen's shoulder a quick kiss, and then sat up. "Lie on your stomach, I want to look at your back."

Gwen did as she was told.

Piper traced several of the lines that made up the mural that was Gwen's large tattoo. "The colors and details of all these birds are magnificent." She placed a kiss on a small bluish bird in the center of Gwen's back. "What's this one hovering in the middle?"

"It's a blue-gray gnatcatcher," Gwen answered.

Piper traced her finger lower. "And this other one hovering is a kingfisher?"

"Yep. You really are learning your birds."

Piper smiled. "This reminds me of the wood carvings all around the boat."

"The carvings were the guide the tattoo artist used when he worked on my back," Gwen said in a low voice.

"How was that possible?" Piper asked.

"Long before I installed the panels on the boat, my tattoo guy used them as a sort of template." Gwen reached down and grabbed the blanket at the foot of the bed, covering them both.

"You installed the panels?" Piper thought about the way Wyatt was able to show her the best way to open the door, and about how Gwen knew the freezer was in the bilge. "This was your family's boat once." She hugged Gwen. "And you are the artist that did all of the wonderful wood carvings. Wow."

Gwen rolled onto her side. Piper kissed her nose. "Tell me about the boat, Gwen."

"What do you want to know?"

"Everything?" Piper asked.

"Well, it was built in nineteen sixty seven. It's forty-one feet long and fourteen feet wide. It weighs upward of about thirty-five thousand pounds."

"That's heavier than non-cement ones?" Piper asked.

"Substantially. It makes it slower and not as responsive in turning, but it's built as strong as a tank. Cement, stainless rebar, and steel mesh, for starters." She laughed. "As Wyatt used to say, 'This ain't no regular backyard built boat. This is the real deal.'"

"I'd never heard of a cement boat before."

"Some of them just have cement hulls. This one is cement in the hull, walls, roof, and gunnels. The only things that aren't cement are the obvious – doors, windows, railings, stuff like that," Gwen explained.

"Thank you," Piper said. "I appreciate you telling me about it. But I would rather kiss you now." She pulled her in for a fierce kiss.

†

Piper was stalking a green heron in the mangroves near the marina when her cell phone vibrated and made her jump. She mostly kept it on in case of an emergency, since she never received calls now that Jeremy had stopped talking to her for her own safety and Gwen, well, Gwen would just stop by here and there, much to Piper's delight.

She answered the phone. "Hello?"

"How's my favorite ex-wife?"

"Jeremy! Oh, my God, it is so good to hear your voice."

Jeremy laughed. "It's good to hear your voice as well. Are you staying out of trouble?"

"Of course." Her gaze slipped toward the ship's store. "How is Anthony?"

"He's good. We're good. And I have some good news for you. The last two of Bronson's goons have been apprehended. That means that Bronson is the only one left."

"That is good news."

"Just don't get any wild ideas about coming home."

She watched Gwen from a distance. "I know. I will stay here where it's safe."

"Huh."

"Huh, what?" Piper asked.

"I expected some resistance from you on that one."

"No, I get it. Bronson is the most dangerous of them all. I know I need to stay put."

"Is there something you aren't telling me?"

"No, it's nothing. This place just isn't as bad as I thought it would be." She played with her camera's menu.

"Did you meet someone?" Jeremy asked.

"No," she lied. She didn't know why, but she wanted to keep Gwen to herself for a while longer. "I've discovered the joys of nature photography. You should see the birds down here, unbelievable."

"Okay, who the hell are you and what have you done with my Piper?"

Piper laughed.

"I shouldn't keep you on the phone too long. It still might not be safe, but I couldn't resist letting you know the good news about the other men being caught."

"I appreciate that. Thank you so much for calling."

†

Gwen looked up when she heard tapping on the window. Wyatt motioned for her to come out. She glanced around the store to be sure there were no customers browsing, then went outside.

"What's up?" she asked.

"Come to my boat for a minute."

"Wyatt, I'm working." She looked around and wished she'd seen more customers milling about.

"It'll only take a second."

"This better not be what I think it is. I told you I'm done."

"Come on, you're wasting time," he said.

She sighed and followed him to the seawall where his boat was tied up. She cringed when she saw Robbie was on it. "I'm not going anywhere with you guys."

"I know. Just get on the boat so we can have some privacy."

Gwen doubted they would have any privacy, but climbed onto the boat. "What's up?"

Wyatt pulled a pillowcase out of the cooler. "Tell me something about this snake."

Gwen looked from Wyatt to Robbie and back to Wyatt. She knew her face must be red with rage. How could Wyatt put her on the spot like that?

"I need you to tell me what it is. It ain't no Burmese." Wyatt opened the case and Gwen peered inside. "What do you think?"

"With that pinkish head, maybe an Indian Python?" Gwen tilted her head and leaned closer to get a better look.

"She don't know what it is," Robbie spat. "Let's just go. I got a dealer that will take this thing." He reached for the pillowcase. Gwen was about to warn him that the head had come to the opening of the case, but hesitated a second and the snake grabbed his arm. Robbie hit the snake on the head and then tried to pull away from it.

"Stop. The more you fight it, the worse it'll be." Gwen shook her head. Robbie tried to act like he knew so much about snakes, yet he didn't seem to know that with their teeth facing backward, you couldn't just pull yourself out of its mouth.

"Can't you tell it to let go," Wyatt whispered to Gwen.

She sighed and gently touched its back. It was all wild, the calmness of just moments ago was gone. "No, I can't."

"Do something!" Robbie screamed. "God damn, that hurts!"

"Stop moving," Gwen told him as she looked around to see if anyone had heard him. "Just stop moving. And keep it down."

"How long you think it'll take?" Wyatt asked her.

"It could be a very long time if he doesn't quit fighting it." She ran her hand partially down the snake's length and tried to gauge its fear. She rested her hand just behind the jaw and concentrated.

"Relax, Rob. Come on, you can do this," Wyatt said.

Robbie took several deep breaths. "Why did it bite me and not you?" he asked Gwen.

"Because you're a dick and I'm not?" Gwen asked.

"Screw you, bitch," Robbie retorted.

"Stop it. Both of you," Wyatt said. "Think of something relaxing to get your mind off the snake," he said to Robbie.

"I can't think with this thing clamped down on me," Robbie whined.

"Hey, remember when Calvin went away to college, and —"

"Stop that, Wyatt," Gwen said as she rolled her eyes at him. She hated that expression that got popular in the eighties after the first round of arrests. Instead of saying so-and-so was away in prison, they'd say he was away at college. As if no one realized they all came back as educated or uneducated as they went in.

Wyatt chuckled. "Just trying to get Robbie's mind off this thing."

Gwen felt a shift in the tingling in her hand and anticipated the snake's next move. At the exact moment it relaxed its jaw, Gwen snatched it away from Robbie's arm. In a fluid movement she had it back in the pillowcase and tied it off. She handed the secured snake to Wyatt. "Do not come near me again with a snake or with this idiot," she said as she nodded toward Robbie. "And make him get a tetanus shot."

"Thanks, Gwen," Wyatt called out to her as she climbed out of the boat and headed back to the store.

She watched them get out of the boat with the snake and go to Wyatt's truck. Robbie had blood dripping down his arm and his face was contorted. *Serves him right*, she thought as she went back inside.

Gwen had to make Wyatt understand that he couldn't come to her for any more help with any snake, for any reason. She was serious about distancing herself from that whole deal. She hated that the snakes were hunted and indiscriminately killed, but she couldn't save the world and the warning from Duane with FWC was all the reason needed. There was no way she was going to let herself get caught up in any legal trouble.

She calmed down as she saw PJ coming off *Ruffled Feathers* and walking down the dock. As she watched PJ through the window, she could almost feel PJ's concentration as she took photos of the pelicans coming in to the seawall.

A throat cleared behind her. Gwen turned. "Hey, Weed, how are you?"

"I'm good," the tall, thin woman said. She pushed an errant strand of her otherwise neatly styled salt and pepper bob behind her ear.

The first time Gwen saw Wendy Sutton, aka Weed, Gwen had been hiking on the Florida National Scenic Trail. She'd gone a bit off the trail when she came across Big Cypress National Preserve's botanist. The woman was doing something to one of the many species of orchids found in the preserve. Gwen asked her questions about what she was doing and was pleasantly surprised when she explained in detail how she was pollinating the plant. She knew that afternoon that she and Weed would be great friends, even if they might go months without seeing one another.

"I haven't seen you around Big Cypress lately," Weed said.

Gwen glanced to where PJ was now taking a picture of crab traps stacked by the seawall. "Yeah, I've been a little busy." She turned back to Weed when she heard her laughing.

"So I see." Weed smiled and her face lit up. "Good for you."

Gwen couldn't help but return the smile.

Weed held up a canvas bag.

"Ah, what have you got there?"

"Cantaloupes from my garden."

"Oh, I love cantaloupes."

Weed laughed. "I know you do." She checked her watch. "I better get going. I'll get the bag from you next time I see you."

Gwen watched for a second as Weed left the store, then her attention returned to PJ. PJ seemed to track a pelican from one boat to another, trying to get a picture. Her gaze followed PJ down the seawall, toward the A-dock.

She needed to get back to work, but couldn't resist the visual feast. Several moments later, she turned her attention to the gas pump when a gentleman pulled his truck and trailered boat up to it. She went outside to unlock the pump and recognized him as the man who had come in wearing all brand new clothing and asking about fishing even though he didn't seem at all interested in her answers. "Hello," she greeted him.

"Hello. Fill up the boat, please." He stood there with his hands in his pockets.

"I'm sorry, we don't pump gas here," Gwen said.

"Oh, don't be ridiculous, sweetheart," Herb boomed from behind her.

"It's your rule," she said, trying to figure out what his angle was. He always had an angle.

"My rule, my changes to the rule. Pump his gas." Herb crossed his arms on his large belly and smiled.

Gwen bit her tongue and did as she was told. *Choose your battles*, as Wyatt said.

After she pumped she watched through the window into the store as the man pulled out a wad of cash. Herb rang the gas up into the register, and then put some of the money in the drawer and some in his pocket. Of course he was wheeling and dealing with this guy. Gwen stayed outside until Herb left through the side door.

She expected the guy to leave now that he had his gas, but he came up to the counter when she went back in the store. "You guys keep these slips pretty much full?"

"Pretty much, especially in season," she answered, referring to the winter months.

"That's a pretty hot Bayliner there."

Gwen looked toward Eric Brown's Command Bridge motor yacht. "Yeah, it's a nice boat."

"Who owns it?" the man asked.

She shrugged, not in the habit of talking about people's property with total strangers.

He nodded. "How about that houseboat on the end, *Ruffled Feathers*? Is that thing seaworthy?"

She shrugged and tried to hide her discomfort.

"Does the owner rent it out?"

She felt the hair stand up on the back of her neck. It wasn't just her being protective of PJ, this guy gave off a dangerous vibe that Gwen couldn't quite put her finger on. "You can leave your phone number and I will find out about the boat for you and have someone give you a call."

He looked at her with narrowed eyes. "Yeah, no, that won't be necessary."

She watched as he got into his truck and pulled out with the small fishing boat she'd just filled up with fuel. It wouldn't hurt her feelings if that guy never came back.

Gwen smiled and nodded when a customer walked up with his bait bucket and asked for three dozen shrimp. She approached the shrimp tank. Her favorite purple-sheened grackle met her there.

"Silly bird," she muttered.

She had just started to scoop the shrimp when she heard the revving of an engine. She glanced behind her but couldn't tell where it was coming from. She finished and handed the bait bucket to the gentleman she was waiting on. The engine sounds revved again. She turned around just in time to see her Uncle Derek's gray Buick driving straight for the boat dock. "What the hell is he doing?" she muttered to herself.

The car turned to the right of the ramp and the engine gunned. The car catapulted right off the seawall.

Gwen dropped the lid to the shrimp tank and sprinted to the boat ramp.

"Hang on, Uncle Derek," she called out. Half way down the ramp her foot hit a patch of the green scum and her legs flew out from under her. She put her hands down behind her to break her fall, but they slipped in the slime and she landed on her left hip and both palms.

She felt more than heard the grunt leave her body with the impact, then tried to right herself, slipping again. She thumped against the side of the seawall and finally got her balance. She half-swam and half-stumbled to the driver's side window.

Her uncle was conscious but confused. He stared at her with his head cocked. At the splashing sound to her left she looked and saw an eleven or twelve-foot alligator moving in her direction. It wasn't Justice. Not getting any kind of vibe off him, she swam to the passenger side window and hoisted herself through it.

"You okay, Uncle Derek?"

He stared at her. His hands gripped the steering wheel. "We just don't talk anymore, Mary Beth."

Gwen swallowed hard. "I know, Derek. I promise I'll try to do better from now on, okay?" She glanced around and saw a spattering of people hanging around, some taking pictures of the car up to its windows in the brackish water.

Derek nodded.

She saw a boat drift to the seawall several yards away. It was Captain Gary. Two men got off the boat, and then Gary drifted back toward them.

"Mary Beth, stay away from my son. He's my blood and I love him, but I don't trust him. Don't think for even a minute that he won't act on his threats."

"What do you mean," she hesitated. "What do you mean, Derek?"

Captain Gary used his bumper pads to cushion between his boat and Derek's car. "Hey, buddy," he said to Derek. "How you doing, pal?"

Derek turned to him and shrugged, an exaggerated, almost comical gesture.

"Can I get you anything?"

"How about a beer?" Derek asked.

Gary chuckled as he reached into his cooler. He handed Derek a Bud Light. "How about you, Gwen, you okay?"

Derek turned to her. "Gwen?"

"Hi, Uncle Derek." He held the beer but didn't move to open it. One hand held the can, the other stayed on his steering wheel with a white knuckled grip.

Gwen could hear the sirens as the rescue squad approached.

†

Piper placed the bag of first aid supplies from the ship's store onto the table on *Ruffled Feathers*. She pulled out packs of gauze and a bottle of alcohol, followed by antibiotic cream and tape.

"You really don't need to go through all this trouble for me," Gwen said.

"It's no trouble. Now let me see your hands."

Gwen placed both hands, palm-side up, onto the table in front of her.

"Do they know why your uncle drove off the seawall? Within seconds of hitting the water the rumors started flying around. They say women are bad gossipers? They have nothing on these old fishermen."

Gwen laughed. Piper opened the alcohol and poured some onto a square of gauze. As soon as she touched Gwen's hand, Gwen stopped laughing.

"Ouch."

"Sorry. So, what do you think happened?" Piper asked.

"He has no business driving, for beginners. He probably got the gas and brake pedals confused."

Piper went about cleaning out the scrapes on Gwen's hands. She briefly ran her thumb along a ridge of callouses that she figured would have been even more pronounced if not for the gloves Gwen often wore when she kayaked. She paused at a small scar on the tissue between her left thumb and index finger. She looked closer and noticed two others near it. "What happened here?"

Gwen glanced down. "Stabbed myself carving wood figurines."

Piper imagined Gwen stabbing herself with a knife or chisel and bringing the wounded hand up to her mouth where she'd absently suck on it as she stared at the piece of wood as it became what it was supposed to become. "Took more than once to learn that lesson, huh?" she teased.

"Yeah. I have two scars on my leg, too. When I was young I used to need to get just the right angle of the blade to compensate for not having really strong hands yet. It only took two times for me to learn not to use my leg for leverage."

"Your parents let you use knives when you were young?"

"I can't remember back to a time when I wasn't allowed to whittle." Gwen shrugged. "I used to do it with my father even before I could walk well."

"You don't talk much about your parents, huh? That night with Wyatt and Robbie was the first time I'd heard anything about them."

Gwen pulled her hand away.

"Sorry," Piper whispered. "I've been told I'm a great listener." She took Gwen's right hand back in hers and used the alcohol drenched gauze to wipe away some concrete particles.

"My parents are both dead."

Piper stopped and looked up. "I thought your mom —"

"Don't believe anything Robbie says. He's an idiot. A hateful idiot." Gwen started to stand but Piper stopped her halfway up. "I'm sorry, PJ. Let's just say, I would bet my own life that my mother is dead."

"I'm sorry. Now sit all the way back down. I need to finish cleaning up your hands."

Gwen sat back down.

"We can't have you getting an infection and losing body parts." Piper held onto Gwen's wrist. "I happen to really like your hands— and what you do to me with those hands." She flipped Gwen's hand and kissed the smooth, undamaged skin there.

"I guess I'll just have to use my mouth."

"Oh, I do like that idea." Piper leaned closer and kissed Gwen lightly on the lips. "You sure you're okay?"

"I'm fine. Really."

"Take your shorts off."

"Wow, my nurse sure did get aggressive," Gwen teased.

"I need to clean the abrasions on your hip. Then I'll need you to show me how you plan to use your mouth."

Gwen lifted an eyebrow, and then stood. "You're in charge." She pulled down her shorts and winced as the material passed across the raw area on her hip.

Piper gently cleaned the area and applied cream and bandaging to it. "I do want to cover up the abrasions on your hands, too. So you won't be tempted to use them."

Gwen held out both hands. "You could always tie me up."

Piper felt a surge of heat move to her groin at the image that resulted. "If I only had some rope or handcuffs," she pouted. She quickly applied the antibiotic cream and gauzed coverings to both hands.

Gwen stood very close to Piper. "So, where were we? Oh, yeah, my mouth, your body. Now I remember."

Piper swallowed hard. "Bed?"

"Yes. Bed." Gwen followed her into the bedroom.

"I want you on your back. Naked, of course. I need to examine every inch of you for any further injuries." Piper pointed at the bed when Gwen didn't immediately obey.

Gwen smiled and Piper helped her remove the rest of her clothing and get situated on her back.

Piper stretched out the length of Gwen, using her arms to keep her weight off of her. She kissed her, softly at first, then harder and deeper. Gwen moaned into her mouth and Piper let her body down just enough to barely touch Gwen's. Gwen arched up to increase the contact.

"You want me?" Piper asked.

"Yes. Please."

Piper kissed down Gwen's neck, slowly down the center of her chest, detouring briefly to kiss each nipple before continuing down her belly. Gwen arched more, gasping.

Once settled between Gwen's thighs, Piper used the fingers of one hand to open her labia, then the fingers on the other to smear the wetness she found there. Gwen tensed, then relaxed into Piper's touch.

"PJ...your mouth...please..."

Piper replaced her fingers with her mouth. She sucked Gwen's clit into her mouth.

"Yes," Gwen said. "Yes." Her hips bucked as Piper kissed, licked, and sucked.

Piper glanced up to see Gwen's hands in the air, obviously trying not to clutch at the sheets as she came.

Gwen's release was fast, and intense. Piper went up to kiss her as soon as her trembling subsided.

"You okay?" Piper asked.

Gwen laughed. "Much, much better than okay."

"How are your hands?"

"What hands?" Gwen teased.

"Let me see."

Gwen held both hands in front of Piper for inspection. Piper was glad to see the bandaging was still intact. The one on her hip, however, hadn't fared as well.

"Wow, how did that happen?" Gwen asked in mock surprise.

"All that bucking around you did." She looked closer. "We need to fix that."

"Not now we don't. Not until after I get to use my mouth on you as promised."

Piper kissed her, and then maneuvered to straddle Gwen's face. "Yes?"

"Oh, yes. Perfect." She quit speaking as Piper lowered herself into position.

Piper groaned as Gwen's lips and tongue found their mark.

Chapter Eleven

Tracy adjusted her black blouse as she walked into the restaurant. She padded her pocket to be sure she had a few ibuprofen tablets for later. *I got this*, she said to herself.

"Hey, Tracy, great to see you," Douglas, the manager, said as she approached the hosting podium. "Britney called in sick. If we get really busy I might need you to serve tonight. Is that okay?"

Tracy smiled at her boss. "Sure, that will be fine."

Serving wasn't her favorite thing, but what's a night here and there? The week before, when Britney had called in sick, she'd enjoyed the interaction with the customers, mostly because it wasn't an ongoing thing. And she had really enjoyed the tips that night.

She remained at the hostess stand for the first thirty minutes of her shift, and then Douglas came to her and asked if she was ready to take a few tables. He planned on seating the customers while she did so.

By the time she'd served drinks to her first table, she regretted her choice of shoes for the evening. The low heel was fine for seating people, but not so comfortable for the back and forth running around required of serving them. She would have to start wearing her more comfortable shoes to work, just in case she ended up filling in for a server.

Tracy was proud of herself for being able to keep up, for learning to pronounce some of the foreign bottles of wine, and for ignoring the steady ache in her bad knee as she worked.

As she passed close to the front of the restaurant, she'd heard Douglas telling someone without a reservation that there was an hour and a half wait. The place was packed and she wasn't even close to being overwhelmed.

Tracy realized that it had been a long time since she'd felt that good about herself.

"Excuse me, ma'am?" A gentleman in a suit and tie called to her.

"Yes, sir."

"Could you tell our server that we're ready to order?" He looked resigned, but not quite angry.

"Yes. Absolutely." She hustled into the back and let Andre know his table was requesting him.

"He's a dick," Andre whispered to Tracy. "And he sucks at tipping."

"How about I take the table some bread and let him know you'll be right there?" Tracy asked.

Andre just grunted. She brought the bread, gave her biggest smile, and promised the gentleman that his server would be right there. He returned her smile as he reached for a chunk of sourdough bread. "Thank you, sweetheart."

She just nodded, ignoring the tone of the word sweetheart, and winked at Andre from across the room.

Anywhere, Everywhere

Table six's salads were ready, so she brought them to the table. It was two couples. One of the women kept sizing Tracy up, leaving Tracy to wonder if she knew her or if maybe that was just how the woman treated all the help. As she placed the Caesar salad in front of the woman she gave her a big smile. "Fresh ground pepper on that?"

The woman stared at her for several moments. "No. Thanks," she finally responded.

Tracy went to the kitchen to wash down two ibuprofen tablets, then moved on to her next table. She tried to ignore the growing ache in her knee. She would have to ice it when she got home.

When she delivered the entrees to the table with the staring woman, she felt even more on display than ever. A gnawing started in her gut. She felt anxiety creeping up her chest and felt panic. Her hand shook as she refilled the woman's water glass.

She rushed to another of her tables where the customers were finishing up their meals. Maybe they would want dessert and she could take an extra few minutes with that. She didn't want to return to table six. She glanced at them as she cleared the dinner plates from the table that was finishing up. The woman watched her and Tracy saw a look of recognition wash over her.

She got the check for that table, and then reluctantly returned to table six to check on them.

"Tracy Snyder," the woman said. She cocked her head. "You don't recognize me, do you?"

Tracy felt that little grain of panic grow into a jagged rock and hated that the next thought she had was how much one little pill would make her feel better. She gave a little shrug. "I'm sorry, I don't."

"From the bank. We worked together briefly as tellers. During my early years, before I became bank president." Her face was growing red, as red as her own must be, Tracy thought.

Tracy turned her attention to the rest of the table. "Can I get you anything else?"

"No, thank you," said the gentleman furthest from the bank president that Tracy still didn't recognize. "Just the check, please."

Tracy smiled and nodded, then backed away from the table, almost bumping into Jordan, one of the bussers. "Sorry," she muttered to him, then made a beeline for the back.

She brought a round of drinks to one of her tables, then the check to table six.

"Here you go," she said, trying to sound as confident as she could. "Whenever you're ready," she added, and then walked away.

A shrill voice from behind her was asking for the manager.

"No," she said to herself. She hid by the corner of the bar and listened. The woman was practically yelling so there was no way not to hear what she was saying to Douglas.

"I refuse to give my credit card to that thief you have working for you. Since when does a fine establishment like this hire junkies? I cannot believe you have that woman working out here, taking people's credit cards. If you have to hire her, at least have the decency to put her in the back washing dishes."

Tracy started to shake uncontrollably. She wanted to bolt out the door, but would not give that woman the satisfaction of doing so. That woman. Denise Holt. Yes, that was her name. And Tracy was pretty sure there was some pretty nasty history between them from when Tracy was using and stealing from anyone and everyone to get her next fix. She fought the urge to throw up.

Tracy went to the restroom and threw cold water on her face. The blood that wasn't pounding in her ears was pounding in her knee. She couldn't stay in there for the rest of the night, but couldn't make herself go out to face the situation for several more minutes. She knew there would be times like this, she had just hoped they wouldn't be so public.

When she went back onto the floor, table six was empty. She heard Andre whisper to another server that Douglas had comped their meal. She busied herself with clearing off one of her tables.

"Tracy."

She looked up to see Douglas motioning to her from the back. She took a deep breath and walked back to him. He led her into the dishwashing area.

"Wow," he said. "That was a first for me."

"Me, too," she said.

"I knew you'd had some problems in the past." He sighed. "I can't have my customers be afraid you'll steal their credit card numbers."

"I would never —"

He held up his hand to stop her. "I don't believe you would. But customer perception is what counts. I promised that woman that you would be dismissed. Otherwise, she said she would be warning everyone in the banking community about coming here."

Tracy felt tears threatening, but held them back.

"I'm sorry, Tracy, but I have to let you go. I'll see that you get your last check mailed to you, as well as any tips still out there for this evening."

She clenched her teeth.

"I'm sorry. I'll walk you out as soon as you get your things."

The next few minutes, as well as the drive to the closest meeting she knew of, were a blur. None of it registered until she sat in the hardback chair and listened to fellow addicts tell their stories.

She took a sip from her bottled water, and then held the cold plastic to her forehead. She should be paying attention to the young man sharing his story, but all she could think was how to tell Wyatt she was fired. And Marion? Would Marion even try to get her another job?

Someone beside Tracy sobbed. Many of the people sitting around her were wiping away tears. Wow, must have been quite a story. She shook her head in an effort to dislodge negativity. Everyone had a story. And every story was important.

The young man who was speaking ended by saying. "Praise God, and I hope you all continue to be blessed."

"Praise God," a few people responded.

She couldn't help but wonder if this guy had traded his drug addiction for a God addiction. She bit the inside of her cheek as punishment. Who was she to judge him or anyone else? She'd mentioned that trade-off to Marion one day. "Well, at least a God addiction won't kill you," Marion had responded.

Tracy took a large gulp from her water as she looked around at everyone. Could she be as strong as these people? Could she finally tell her story out loud?

"Would anyone else like to share?" a voice to her right asked.

"Um," Tracy started. Then she changed her mind. Everyone was staring at her.

"Go ahead," someone urged her.

She looked around. They were all looking at her anyway, so why not share. Besides, it couldn't be as traumatizing as her last few minutes at work.

"I'm Tracy," she started.

"A little louder, please."

"I'm Tracy, and I'm an addict. I've been clean for almost four months."

A few people gave a quick clap or two for her, catching her off guard. These meetings were all so different, she never knew what to expect.

"I got addicted to pain pills after hurting my knee. One thing led to another and before I knew it I wasn't just skimming time off my dosing but also injecting heroin." She took a deep breath to calm herself. "I lied to everyone in my life. I stole from people I cared the most about. Once," she took a deep breath. "Once I even had sex with someone for a few pills."

She glanced around and found no looks of judgement.

"I'm clean and trying to rebuild those relationships that I screwed up. But even with a little weight on, even with my hair filling back in, even with my new teeth," she gestured with her finger to her partial plate, "Even with the outside looking normal again, I still feel like a fraud sitting here."

A woman across from her nodded her acknowledgement.

"On the inside I'm still a thief, and a liar, and an addict, just looking for an excuse to use again." Her breathing grew rapid. "And every time I come to a meeting full of praise God's and halleluiah's, I feel like a double fraud because I think you people are fooling yourselves by relying on God to get you through. It's just a crutch you use, but at least you have it to use, and how am I going to make it through without faith in your false deity?"

She stood up and knocked her chair over. The guy beside her also stood.

"I'm sorry," she sobbed.

A pair of arms embraced her and a calm voice said, "It's okay to feel that way. Many of us have felt the very same way at one point or another."

She shook. The shaking made her think of detoxing at the community hospital four months earlier. At least there she'd had a bed with blankets. The first couple of times she detoxed she did so in jail, with only a mattress and blood pressure pills.

"Now, why don't you sit back down?" He gestured around the room. "We're all in this together."

She forced herself to sit in her now upright chair. She stared at the floor, unable to look anyone in the eyes for the rest of the meeting. Afterward, she left without a word.

Once at home, she stood in front of the mirror and said her affirmations.

"You are a kind, loving person. You are deserving of love and kindness. Your inner beauty shines brightly. You are strong." She laughed out loud at the absurdity of her words. She hadn't felt like a kind loving person while she was raging at those poor people in that meeting. She sighed. She had to do it again, and again, until she believed it.

"You are a kind, loving person. You are deserving of love and kindness. Your inner beauty shines brightly. You are strong."

She left the bathroom and grabbed the ice pack from the freezer and the bottle of Ibuprofen from the counter, then sat with her leg up and the ice on her knee. She washed down two tablets, the only thing she allowed herself to take for the pain, even though it barely took the edge off.

"What now?" she asked herself. "What do I do now?"

She wondered if Gwen could get her a job at the marina store, but knew she wouldn't even ask. She had to do this on her own. She could not let Wyatt or Gwen know what had happened at Newman's Steak House that night.

†

Piper pulled Gwen closer. It had been a very long time since she'd woken up next to someone in the morning. And an even longer time since she'd had such a great night. Maybe she'd never had such a great night. Since she was having a difficult time thinking of such a time, she decided she hadn't ever had a night as wonderful as the one she'd just shared with Gwen.

Very little light shone into the bedroom, so Piper decided it must be quite early. She wanted to check the time on her watch on the bedside table, but didn't want to wake up Gwen. Then she heard a noise and found herself bolting into a sitting position, waking Gwen up anyway.

"What's wrong?" Gwen asked as she rolled to face her.

"Someone is outside the boat." She pulled the covers up to her neck. There was another noise.

"Want me to check it out?"

"No. It's not safe," Piper whispered. "Besides, what about your hands?"

"It's probably just a critter. If it'll make you feel better, I'll go check," Gwen said as she got out of bed. She cocked her head. "I seriously doubt it's anything. I'll just stick my head out the door to make sure. Okay?"

Piper felt foolish. Then she heard the noise again, only louder.

Gwen slipped into her shorts, wincing as the material went across her hip. Then she slowly pulled on her tank top. "My hands feel remarkably well. Must be the excellent medical treatment I received." She smiled, and then went outside.

Piper got out of bed and pulled the curtain to the side. She watched as a small motor boat came from beside the dock, near her slip.

She heard Gwen as she rushed back inside, but kept her eyes on the man in the boat. The image from that dark alley assaulted her. Then she remembered…she remembered being bent over the table, Gwen filling her from behind, and it not quite registering. She snatched her hand away from the curtain and spun around to face Gwen.

"I don't know what that was all about, but the boat is gone now. Probably someone thinking maybe *Ruffled Feathers* was empty and they would come aboard and help themselves to your...PJ? PJ, you're white as a sheet."

Piper felt her hands shaking. She looked down at them and then back up at Gwen. "Bronson. That was Bronson. He's found me. Oh, my God, what do I do now?"

"What are you talking about? Do you know that guy out there? You've seen him before?"

"I saw him the first night we, ah, we had sex. Through the window by the table. But it didn't quite register at the time. The way he was dressed.... Part of me assumed it was one of your drug guys. I don't know!"

"One of my drug guys? What in the hell are you talking about?" Gwen asked.

"Oh, come on, I've been watching you handing off sacks of drugs to Wyatt," Piper said.

"Stop. Just stop. It's not drugs, it's —" She took a step back. "Wait a minute, back up. Who is Bronson and why does it matter that he's found you?"

"It all started when I got bored filming weddings and decided I should become a photojournalist. My first attempt was of a deal going down between this Bronson guy and some other dude." Piper shivered.

"What happened, PJ?"

"I got the perfect photo of Bronson shooting the other guy in the head."

"Whoa." Gwen took a step back. "And he found out?"

"I sold the story and photo to the newspaper. He and his thugs were supposed to be behind bars before the paper printed the story." She shrugged. "Not so bright on my part, huh?"

"And now you're hiding," Gwen stated. "Wow."

"And apparently not doing such a great job of hiding since Bronson found me."

"We should call the cops," Gwen said.

"I don't know who to trust. Bronson's got deep pockets, what if he's already got someone in local law enforcement working for him?"

Gwen breathed in deeply. "I understand your reluctance to involve the police. We'll figure something out, but come to my place in the meantime."

Piper paced the short area of the boat. "That will put you in danger. Shit, I've already put you in danger by having you here with me."

Gwen grabbed Piper's arm, then immediately released it with a wince.

"Your hand."

"It's fine. And I'm here because I've chosen to be. I'm not going anywhere. We just need to concentrate on keeping you safe." She pulled Piper in for a hug.

†

Gwen handed the shot gun to PJ and thought of the slip of paper that Captain Gary had given her with the number of the retired FBI agent. Did she dare trust this guy?

She double-checked that all the windows were locked. She moved the table to the side to be sure the door it was blocking was also locked.

"Whoa, that's a door?" PJ asked.

"Ah, yeah." Gwen gestured toward the lock. "It's secure." She moved the table back in position in front of the door.

PJ shrugged. "It never occurred to me that it was anything other than a window."

"Hey, PJ, I need you to know something."

PJ cocked her head.

"Wyatt and I are not dealing drugs. We've been catching exotic snakes and taking out the nice ones before they can be hunted."

"Exotic snakes? I have no idea what you're talking about," PJ admitted.

"I'll explain it better later, after we get this situation with that Bronson guy taken care of." Gwen leaned closer and kissed her on the cheek.

"Okay."

"It's just important to me that you know I would never deal drugs," Gwen said.

She left PJ with the shotgun in ready position. "Please, don't shoot yourself."

"I'll be careful."

"I'm just going to make some calls to see where we can hide you until we figure out a plan." She looked at PJ, saw how scared she was, and felt herself go into protector mode.

Gwen stood by the mangroves where she could get a signal and keep her eye on *Ruffled Feathers* and PJ. She'd known the woman was hiding something from her but never would have guessed this.

She dialed Weed to see if she still kept in touch with the camp owner up off of Concho Billie, an off road vehicle trail in Big Cypress National Preserve. An outsider would never be able to find PJ there. And she figured most folks from that area wouldn't embrace a stranger like him too quickly. A lot of the older guys in both Everglades City and Big Cypress didn't trust easily.

Weed was sweet about not getting the whole story, and told Gwen she'd arrange for a buddy's swamp buggy to take Gwen and PJ out to the camp the next day.

She hung up the phone with Weed and started to walk back to the boat. She glanced around to see if she'd see Wyatt. She wanted to talk to her brother about what was going on with PJ. She'd barely seen him since she told him she wouldn't grab snakes with him anymore. And with Tracy back in the picture, she saw him even less.

She didn't see Wyatt, but did see Tracy, behind the ship's store, talking to Robbie. "No way. Not again," Gwen muttered. Now she had two things she really needed to talk to Wyatt about.

She checked her watch. She had to go to work. She'd be the only one in for the day and couldn't call out sick. She had given PJ instructions to stay put while she worked, and Gwen would keep an eye on the boat. Once she found Wyatt, she would have him go to make sure all was well at *Ruffled Feathers* until she got off work. Her plan was to stay with PJ for the night, then they would hide her out in the swamp until they came up with a definitive plan.

Once she had PJ tucked somewhere safe, she would give serious consideration to calling Dale Townsend, the retired FBI agent.

Chapter Twelve

"Why you limping?" Wyatt asked.

"My knee hurts," Tracy said.

"What's up with your knee?"

It infuriated her that he even had to ask, that he couldn't connect the dots for himself after all these years. "You know, back when we were together and I fell in your truck and screwed up my knee, then got addicted to pain pills, and eventually anything else I could get my hands on." She glared at him, unable to curb her anger. "You know, the stupid little accident in the back of your truck that screwed up my entire life?"

"Oh." He looked away. "We need to talk."

"Wonderful."

"Seriously, Trace, I saw you talking to Robbie earlier."

She took a deep breath. "I didn't buy anything from Robbie."

"But you were thinking about it," Wyatt said.

"And yet, I didn't!" She had no right to expect Wyatt to understand addiction, but it didn't keep her from growing angry at him. "I am a recovering addict, Wyatt. I can't change that. And I can't help it if I think about using every now and then. But thinking is not the same as doing. And giving me shit for thinking about it isn't helping the situation."

"No, Tracy, you aren't allowed to even think about it. Because I know where that will lead," Wyatt said.

"That's not being very supportive."

He shook his head. "I will not sit back and watch you do that to yourself again. No fucking way."

Tracy watched helplessly as he stormed away. *Suit yourself.*

She walked toward the ship's store, but didn't go in. She paced the length of the sidewalk outside the store and knew she should get in her truck and go to a meeting. There was a meeting off of Pine Ridge where she'd never been. It would be nice, after her outburst at the last meeting, to start anew at a different location.

"Get in your truck and drive away," she whispered to herself as she glanced around to see if Robbie was still hanging out at the marina. "You are stronger than your craving." Her knee started throbbing even more than its usual pain, almost like it was taunting her. She flinched as she stepped wrong and pain shot through the joint.

She considered calling Marion, but didn't want to admit to her sponsor that she was even considering a pill or two. Marion would be so disappointed. Tracy's father would sever the very last tie if he ever found out. But at least Tracy could hush the craving long enough to figure out her next step, decide what to do about work, and life in general.

Tracy headed to the far side of the seawall where she'd last seen Robbie. When Robbie approached, her heart started pounding. She was excited. It would all be okay. She just needed a few pills to take the edge off. Then, once she felt better, she could concentrate on getting Wyatt back and getting clean. There were other folks at her meetings who'd given in and were able to recover just fine from it. It'd be no problem for her either.

She tucked the four pills into her pocket after giving Robbie a soggy stack of ones, the last of her tips from waitressing the night she got fired. Once her knee felt better, she would be able to concentrate on finding another job. She just needed a little relief first.

Tracy heard Wyatt's voice and turned to see him talking to some old fisherman. She made a beeline for the ship's store. She was relieved when she saw the cooler door propped open, meaning Gwen was busy in there. She made her way to the back of the store and slipped into the women's restroom. She had an idea, so she went back out and to the souvenir section and found what she was looking for – the collector spoons that she'd figured had gone out of style years earlier. These had the image of a manatee etched onto them. She snatched up two. She laughed. It was almost too easy.

She returned to the bathroom and went into the handicapped stall. She used one spoon to crush two pills against the second spoon. She smiled right before snorting first one half, then the other. "Now, I got this," she said. "It'll be okay now with the edge off."

Feeling instantly better, she sat on the edge of the toilet, not caring that she might get her shorts dirty from the toilet seat. The warm, relaxed sensation started at the back of her legs, making her smile. Euphoria engulfed her. She felt warm and perfectly at peace. She opened her hand, looking for the other two pills, wondering if she'd taken them already. She leaned forward to see if she'd dropped them on the floor. She didn't see them, but she stayed in that position for a long time, enjoying the euphoria. She let out a contented sigh just before falling onto the floor. The initial contact sent a jolt through her head, but then the tile felt nice and cool on her face. *Everything is okay now. I got this.*

†

Gwen was watching the houseboat from the doorway of the store when her brother walked up to her. She was about to start telling him what was going on with PJ and Bronson when he spoke quickly. "Where's Tracy?"

"She's not with you?" Gwen took a deep breath. "We need to talk, Wy."

"No, we don't," he said.

"Yes, we do. For beginners, I think Tracy's using again."

"I know," Wyatt's voice broke and Gwen's heart broke along with it.

"I'm sorry," Gwen whispered.

He nodded, and then turned away. "If you see her, give me a shout."

"Okay." She watched him walk away, hating how he slouched in his despair.

She went inside and straightened the candy bar rack, then the chips. She glanced out the window and saw Wyatt chatting with Peter. She wondered if it was early enough in Tracy's fall from the wagon to keep her from hitting rock bottom again.

It hurt her to see Wyatt in pain and she'd really hoped Tracy would stay clean this time, not just for Wyatt but also for Tracy's sake. Gwen liked Tracy and wished for her to succeed in beating the monster of addiction.

She looked up at the sound of a knock on the window. Pete stood there, gesturing toward the gas pumps. She went out to unlock them.

"Go ahead and fill her up," Pete said.

"Not in this lifetime." She snuck another glance at the PJ's boat and saw nothing out of the ordinary.

She unlocked the padlock, then slipped it onto her belt loop since if she left it at the pumps it tended to walk off. She hoped Wyatt would come into the store after she finished dealing with Peter so she could have a quiet moment to talk to him about PJ's predicament.

She'd just turned away from the pump when a tourist who had been waiting for her eco-tour to begin came running out of the store. "I need help!" She waved her arms at Gwen. "Some woman is passed out on the bathroom floor!"

Gwen knew instantly who it was. As she took off in a sprint, she could sense Wyatt right on her heels.

She saw legs sticking out from under the handicap stall, but the door was shut and locked. She slid under the door and stood to unlock it. Wyatt catapulted through the door as soon as it opened.

Gwen couldn't help focusing on the drool drying around Tracy's mouth. She reached out and felt for a pulse. "I don't feel anything."

"CPR, do CPR," Wyatt begged.

She stood there, feeling helpless, not even remembering the first thing about administering CPR. Then she watched as PJ knelt beside Tracy and turned her so that she was flat on her back. "Tracy, Tracy?" She adjusted Tracy's head and opened her mouth.

"Don't die, Tracy, please don't die," Wyatt started chanting in the door to the stall.

PJ administered CPR until two paramedics arrived. They performed CPR for several moments, and then loaded her onto a gurney. Gwen studied their faces and she knew that taking her in the ambulance was mostly for show. Tracy was already gone.

She slumped onto the floor, her back against the wall, and allowed PJ to embrace her. "What are you doing off the boat?" she sobbed.

"I heard the ruckus and got scared that something bad had happened to you," PJ whispered.

"She's not going to live," Gwen said. "I know with every cell in my body that she's gone."

"I am so sorry," PJ responded.

Chapter Thirteen

Piper sat in Wyatt's truck with him and reflected on Tracy's death. She felt so bad for both Wyatt and Gwen. What could Piper possibly say to Wyatt that wouldn't sound lame?

Gwen had told Piper earlier that Tracy's father refused to claim her body. That made Piper so very sad. The folks around the marina and ship's store had started taking up a collection. This community was willing to help Wyatt be able to afford to have Tracy cremated so she didn't have to spend eternity in the ground, the last place, she'd told Wyatt more than once, that she wanted to end up.

She closed her eyes and the image of Tracy on the bathroom floor assaulted her. Just like the image of Bronson's victim had for all this time, this, she was sure, would haunt her for the rest of her life.

She glanced at Wyatt and noticed he had an unnatural grip on the steering wheel, almost like he was holding on for dear life. He probably was, she thought.

"I appreciate you helping me with my problem," Piper said. "With all you have going on, I know this must be the last thing you wanted to do today."

He nodded. "It's okay," he said, his voice not much more than a croak.

"We're going to a hunting camp in the swamp?" she asked.

"Yeah. A friend of a friend." He looked around one last time before pulling onto Tamiami Trail and heading east. "Just until we figure this out." His grip on the steering wheel relaxed a little. "Gwen's going to call that retired FBI guy we talked about."

Piper nodded. She wondered if having her problem to think about was helping Wyatt cope.

"We might hit some rain," he said absently.

Piper leaned so she could see the sky above them better. "Yeah, looks like it." She closed her eyes for a moment, until she saw Tracy on the floor again, then opened them. She could feel the pressure of Tracy's rigid mouth against hers as she tried to breath for her. She could smell the rancidness of the vomit on Tracy's face.

"You okay?" Wyatt asked. "You don't look so good."

"I'm fine," she said. How do you tell someone that the image of their dying girlfriend made you momentarily feel sick? "How about you? You okay?"

He gave her such a blank look that she shuddered. "I'm cool."

Piper remembered the flash drive with the pictures of Gwen that she'd left on the boat. She had no idea what would happen next, or if she'd ever make it back to *Ruffled Feathers*. She was fine with losing all her clothes, and her camera, but she couldn't stand the idea of not having the pictures of Gwen when this was all over. "Wyatt, can we please go back to the boat?"

"To *Ruffled Feathers*?" He checked his watch.

"It will only take a minute. I forgot something important."

Wyatt nodded, and then turned the truck around. "When we get there, you take my pistol in with you. I'm gonna stay in the truck and be ready to get the hell out of there once you come out."

She glanced down at the pistol on the bench seat between them. The rifle was stuffed behind the truck seat, just out of sight.

†

Gwen had just finished installing a camera inside and to the left of the door when she stepped down off the chair she'd pulled over, onto the rug covering the bilge's trapdoor. She'd used her pocket knife to shimmy the lock on the boat, having just come up with the idea to install the camera and watch the boat via her laptop. She stood in the middle of the living area of *Ruffled Feathers*. She stared at the trapdoor leading down to the bilge… to the freezer. Tears coursed down her cheeks as she heard her mother's words, as vivid as if she was standing right in front of Gwen.

"Gwenny, I've hidden something in the freezer. If I don't come back tonight, you get the envelope out and give it to the investigator with the long mustache. Okay?"

Gwen shook as she realized her mother hadn't told her to hide in the freezer, after all. No wonder none of it made sense to her back then, or during all the years that had passed. She wasn't supposed to hide in the freezer.

She saw herself at seven years old, small for her age, but still too big to truly hide in there. She'd crouched there, the door open, the power turned off, waiting until her Uncle Derek found her.

"Child, what in God's name are you doing in there?" he'd asked. "And why are you carrying on crying like that?" He'd pulled her out and handed her up to another man, a crabber who worked with her uncle and father. Both men had joined her father in prison within a month. Both had served a little time and returned to Everglades to resume their lives... like so many others, just not Luke Martin.

Gwen fought to control her breathing as she stared at the rug covering the bilge door. She pulled it to the side and yanked the door open. Her legs shook as she lowered herself down, landing next to the freezer. She opened the freezer and started pulling out frozen dinners and popsicles. She threw the food onto the floor, covering her feet. Once the freezer was empty, she started poking at the bottom of it. It gave, a lot, too much to be normal, she was sure. She stuck the blade of her pocket knife in the corner and pried the false bottom up. Hidden below the false bottom was a sealed freezer bag with a thick envelope in it.

A shadow cast over Gwen from above and she jumped. She looked up and saw Piper pointing a pistol at her.

"What in the hell are you doing?" Piper asked, obviously confused and concerned.

"Put that thing away. Please." She held her breath until Piper lowered the gun.

As Gwen climbed out of the bilge, Wyatt came storming through the door. "They're watching us from one of the outside hotel rooms." He looked at Gwen, undoubtedly noticing her tear streaked face. "What is going on? What the hell are you doing here? You were supposed to meet us at the trail head when you got off work."

"I just remembered something." She felt disconnected, as if she were drifting. "I didn't know what it was. I couldn't *not* come here, you know? I realized when I came inside that I had it wrong back then. Mom didn't tell me to hide in the freezer. She told me she'd hidden something in the freezer." She held up the bagged envelope.

Wyatt reached for it but Gwen held it against her chest. He cocked his head. "We can't worry about that right now. Bronson, or whoever the hell he is, has been watching us. If we go to the camp now, they'll follow us. We need a plan."

Gwen relaxed a little when PJ came up behind her and wrapped her arms around her. Gwen clasped her hand in her free one.

"I had a piece of a plan," Gwen said, shaking her head as if to bring herself back to the present. She pointed up to the camera. "At least now, if something happens on board, we'll have proof of who did it."

They all jumped at the sound of thunder. Wyatt laughed. "We're a bunch of wusses," he said. "Okay. Give me a minute to think about this." He stroked the small patch of whiskers just below his bottom lip. "Let me think about this," he said, distracted.

Gwen watched as Wyatt's face contorted. She wondered if this was a good distraction, or if putting off his grief about Tracy's death would just make it worse when it finally hit him. She couldn't help worrying how his girlfriend's death would affect him once it truly sank in.

Rain started to pelt the boat. "I have a plan," Wyatt announced. "But we should wait until dark and hope like hell the rain keeps on coming."

†

Jagged, bright streaks sliced through the black sky as Wyatt walked onto the dock.

PJ kept her hooded head low as the rain pelted her yellow slicker as she stepped away from *Ruffled Feathers*. "Hurry up, Gwen. We gotta get out of here," Wyatt said loudly to PJ as she walked toward him. She waved Wyatt off, then her left sandal lost its grip but she managed not to fall.

Wyatt turned back to the figure standing in the boat's doorway wearing shorts, a T-shirt, and a ball cap. "PJ, stay inside and don't open the door for anyone but me or Gwen. Now get inside and stay inside."

Gwen closed the door to the houseboat and locked it. She hoped like hell the men watching bought it and believed it was PJ inside, not Gwen. Her heart pounded as she peeked out the side of the window and watched her two favorite people walking down the wet dock.

"Stay safe," she whispered.

Gwen looked again and saw Wyatt standing beside his truck. She heard him call out to PJ. "Come on, Gwen, hurry up. The weather's getting worse." Then she heard the engine start and the truck pull away.

Anywhere, Everywhere

Gwen yanked off the ball cap and kicked off her sandals. She double-checked that the envelope in the plastic bag was securely taped to her torso. It was taped and wrapped in a layer of plastic wrap. She hoped it would be enough to protect the contents, because she wasn't willing to let it out of her sight for even a moment. She glanced toward the bedroom door, half-closed, where they had made up the bed to look like someone was asleep under the covers.

She slid the table away from the door it had been blocking and peeked through the space between the curtain panels. She didn't see anyone, couldn't hear anything. She opened the door just a crack and looked again. She listened intently, but still heard nothing but the rumble of thunder and impact of rain. She hoped it wasn't hiding anything she needed to hear.

Gwen twisted her body to fit through the small opening she'd made when she slid the door partially opened. She struggled at first to slide the mostly unused door shut behind her before squatting on the gunnel. She glanced around, and then ducked under the aluminum railing. She held on to the edge of the side of the boat and gently lowered herself down, slipping quietly into the dark, brackish water. Her senses came alive, in that way that can only happen when you leave yourself that vulnerable, alone in the dark water.

The water was rough and the wind disorienting. Her head was the only part of her above water. She closed her eyes and tried to focus on picking up any energy that might be in the water with her. There was no sense in swimming right up to a hungry alligator if she could prevent it. She felt a cold indifference coming from the edge of the mangroves, but nothing from the direction of the other side of the marina where she wanted to go.

She swam underwater, only coming up for air a few times before she got to the slip she'd chosen. Carl Wilson was out of town for a month or longer, so hiding on his boat would be a good choice. She slipped up beside it and hung on to the edge of the dock while she listened for any sign that she'd been noticed. Her entire body tensed up when she felt the hostile energy propelling through the water toward her. Then she felt, more than saw, a presence around her. The size of the mass on either side of her cemented her knowledge that she had a manatee on each side. The alligator aborted its approach to her and she hoisted herself onto the dock as she gave a silent thank you to her protectors.

She felt the sting on her palms then as the still tender flesh of her hands grasped the edge of the rough wood of the dock. "Shit," she whispered. Then she chastised herself for making even that slight sound. She looked around her once more, struggling to see in the pouring rain, and then slipped under the cover of Carl's Boston Whaler, where she sprawled, making herself as flat as she could, and waited for whatever was going to happen to happen.

She figured she would mix in with a group of tourists as they arrived the next morning for their eco tours. That was, unless something big happened during the night. She shuddered at the thought of what might have happened to PJ had they not figured out that this Bronson guy was on to her.

The pressure of the envelope from the freezer against her torso kept her mind lingering on the edge of thoughts about what she might find out about her mom's death. What if it was nothing? What if she was no closer to learning the truth? Could she live with not knowing the real story?

The boat rocked in the wind and made Gwen feel a little queasy. She had just started to drift off when a loud noise jarred her. *What the hell?* She rolled her shoulders, trying to work a kink out before she stuck her head out from under the corner of the boat cover. She studied the silhouette of *Ruffled Feathers* against a slight orange glow from the early morning light. A sudden explosion blew a hole in the side of the boat. She gasped, her breath catching in her chest. She'd known they would do something, but didn't think it would be that.

Memories of years spent on that boat as a child flashed through her mind... of the hard work she put into its renovation...and of making love to PJ there.

Dark smoke poured through the blown out windows and doors, billowed out of the gaping hole that was jagged with twisted rebar. The slight orange glow of morning was now the brighter orange of flames.

There was a flurry of activity around the hotel and the store. This gave Gwen an opportunity to really make it look good. She jumped out of the boat and ran through the parking lot, behind the ship's store and along the sea wall, yelling.

"PJ... oh, God, PJ!" As she approached the B-dock, Peter intercepted her. "Let me go, PJ is in there!"

"No one is in there anymore," he said. "Not alive anyway."

Gwen stood next to Peter, allowing him to put a sympathetic arm around her shoulder, and watched as the boat that had meant so much to her family darkened with soot, and then sank. She could hear the sirens approaching. They screamed like the anguish in her head.

Chapter Fourteen

Piper stood in Gwen's wood shop, looking at all the saws and a few hand tools. There was an entire cabinet of pieces of driftwood, wood panels, and blocks of wood. She could picture the concentration that must have been on Gwen's face as she brought each piece of wood to life.

She turned to see Gwen and Wyatt standing in the doorway. She rushed toward them and they all embraced. "What's going on?" she asked, desperate to know.

"They blew her up," Gwen whispered.

"What?" Piper asked.

"They blew up *Ruffled Feathers*."

Wyatt stood beside his sister, his expression blank. Piper wondered if this was where it would all sink in, the loss of the boat driving home the reality of the loss of Tracy.

"What now?" Piper asked.

"There is a crew working to bring up what they can of the boat. The forensics team is working on the dock now." Wyatt sat on a stool. "You need to decide now if you are dead or alive."

"What?"

"Do you fake your death and start over, or go to the authorities and tell them you are alive?" Gwen asked.

"What do you think I should do?" Piper asked Gwen.

"That's got to be your decision." Gwen pulled her into a hug as she spoke. "No one can tell you what to do next."

"But I really do want to know what you would do."

Gwen nodded. "I would go to the authorities. The truth will set you free, right?" She pressed against the envelope still taped to her side. "I know one truth I'm ready for."

"Yes, let's finally get to that. Then later I will go to the police and let them know I'm okay." She squeezed Gwen's shoulder. "We have video of them doing whatever they did to the boat, right?"

"Sure do," Wyatt said.

"So they go to jail and I'm home free," Piper said.

Wyatt nodded again, his expression still unreadable.

"PJ isn't your real name, is it?" Gwen asked. "Do we get to know your real name now?"

"It's Piper. Piper Jackson."

Wyatt studied her. "I think I'll stick to PJ. No offense."

"No offense taken." She turned to Gwen with raised eyebrows. "You ready?" she asked as she gestured toward Gwen's torso.

Gwen pulled up her shirt and carefully separated the tape from her skin. Piper had to keep from reaching to assist. Gwen carefully removed a large manila envelope from the sealed freezer bag. She pulled out a stack of letters and a mini cassette. She leafed through the letters and noted they were all signed by someone using R as a signature.

"Who even has one of those players anymore?" Piper asked, not really expecting an answer.

"I do," Gwen whispered. "In the box of my mom's things."

Wyatt stepped forward. "You have a box of her stuff?"

"Aunt Linda gave it to me when I left for college. There was a mini cassette player and one unopened cassette." She looked toward the corner of the shop. "Do you think the cassette will still work after being in the freezer?"

"Only one way to find out," Wyatt said. "Where's the box?"

Gwen walked to the far corner and crouched down. She slid a cardboard box, about two-feet by three-feet, out from under the bottom shelf. Wyatt moved in closer to see as Gwen opened the box.

From behind them, Piper glanced at the photos, their mom's locket, her drivers' license.

Gwen picked up the small, outdated recording device. She hit the power button but nothing happened.

Wyatt took it from her and opened the back. "Needs batteries."

"I have some in the house, I think."

"Well, go get them while I look at the letters," Wyatt said.

"No," Gwen took a deep breath. "We look at the letters together. Then we'll go get batteries and listen, together."

"Gimme," Wyatt said as he reached for the letters.

Gwen slapped his hand away. "Quit grabbing, you'll rip one." She unfolded them and started arranging them by date.

"They're all handwritten?" Piper asked.

"Yeah, so far." Gwen held a letter at different angles. "Might not be able to read all of it, the writing is so bad."

"Who they from?" Wyatt asked.

"R," Gwen answered.

"R?"

"Roy Crews?" Gwen whispered. "They're love letters." Gwen looked at Wyatt, then Piper. "Here it says, *I know you think I'm too young for you, but love don't know age.*" Gwen gave an exaggerated shiver.

Wyatt held out his hand and Gwen handed the top letter to him.

"Shit," Wyatt said. "Listen to this. *It don't matter that you're my aunt. If this was a hundred years ago it would be everyday stuff.*"

"R is Robbie? That idiot was in love with my mother?" Gwen asked.

"I think I just threw up in my mouth," Wyatt said.

Gwen looked at Piper. "How's that for some family history?" she asked. She held up one, offering it to her. Piper took it from her and started reading.

"This one turns threatening," Piper said after a few minutes of reading. "Robbie is threatening her. Says if she says anything to anyone about what he told her, he would kill her."

Gwen read out from another one. "*I love you and if I can't have you, no one can.*"

"Do you think he killed your mother in a lover's rage?" Piper asked.

"In an unrequited lover's rage, maybe. But there is no way my mother had anything to do with that creep in a romantic way. No way."

"Our mother," Wyatt whispered.

"What?" Gwen asked.

"Our mother. You say 'my mother' so much that sometimes I think you forget that she was my mother, too."

Gwen reached for Wyatt but he pulled away.

"Don't get touchy feely on me. I want to listen to the cassette tape. We done with the letters?"

"Wyatt." Gwen's voice was so low it caused both Wyatt and PJ to lean closer. "This one is from Mom, to us."

"*Hi kids. If you are reading this then something has happened to me. Give these letters and this tape to Roy Crews. He's a private investigator who has been looking for a missing person, and I've been helping him with it. You can trust him. When your dad gets home he will need you so very much. Listen to him, he's a smart man and great father. Take care of one another, okay? I love you with all of my heart. Love, Mom.*"

They were quiet for several moments. Then Gwen silently folded the letter and set it on the workbench. "Here's the last one from Robbie to Mom."

Wyatt gestured for her to read it. She did so to herself for a minute, and then read aloud. "*Meet me at our island.*" Gwen stopped reading and looked up. "I wonder which island was theirs." She gave an exaggerated shiver. "*And I'll show you where I hid his body.*"

"Whoa, what the hell?" Wyatt asked. "The tape. I bet the answers are on that tape."

The three gathered up the letters and the box of Mary Beth Martin's belongings and went into Gwen's small house.

Wyatt closed the door behind them, then as an afterthought locked it.

Piper stepped into the den and focused on a photo displayed on a small table while Gwen rooted around looking for batteries. The picture was of Gwen's entire family. She must have been only three or four years old. Piper wanted to go pick it up, study it, but couldn't bring herself to do it. She looked at Wyatt and was embarrassed that he'd caught her staring at the photo.

"Gwen made that frame," he said.

Now Piper couldn't resist. She moved closer and picked it up. There were engravings of all kinds of fish, several dolphins, a manatee, and an osprey.

"Here are the batteries," Gwen said as she came in to the room from the kitchen. She gave Piper a sad smile as Piper replaced the picture onto the table.

"Gimme," Wyatt said. Gwen rolled her eyes at him but then handed him several batteries. Both women watched as he shoved the batteries into the back and replaced the plastic cover holding them in place. "Ready?" he asked.

Gwen took Piper's hand. "Yes, ready."

Wyatt pressed the play button. Nothing happened, so he tapped it against the palm of his hand. A voice boomed out. "Thanks for meeting me."

"That's Robbie," Wyatt said.

"Shh!" Gwen admonished.

"Robbie, stop," Mrs. Martin's voice said.

"What? Can't a guy hug his favorite aunt?"

Piper looked at Gwen and thought she might get sick. She squeezed her hand, and Gwen squeezed back.

"You were going to tell me about the Jones boy," Mary Beth said.

"I don't know why you're so interested in that kid. He wasn't anyone really."

A sound echoed, as if they were walking in the wind now. "You're the one who started telling me about him."

"Only because you weren't taking me seriously."

"Of course, I take you seriously. Now, tell me what happened next. You found some coke and you and Tommy Jones snorted some?"

"Yeah. He was a young kid whose family had just moved to the area. I took him under my wing, if you know what I mean," Robbie said.

"So, he snorted too much and died?"

"Yep. It was an accident, sort of. I wanted to know how much coke he'd have to snort for it to kill him."

"You said the other day that you forced him to snort it. How did you do that?"

Robbie's laugh boomed out of the speaker. "By putting a gun to his head, of course. What, are you writing a book?"

Piper grew nervous, afraid that he'd figured out Mary Beth was taping him.

"Was he afraid?" Mary Beth asked, not missing a beat.

"He was, until he didn't know any better any more. He cried. Said he felt sick and didn't want to do any more."

"Did you ever think to stop?" Mary Beth asked.

"Nah, not really. Afterward, I was sorry."

"You were?" Piper could hear a hopeful tone in Mary Beth's words.

"Yeah, I was sorry. I could have made a bunch of money on what I wasted on him."

"So, what happened next?" Mary Beth's voice was low.

"Next?" Robbie asked.

"After you kept forcing him to snort more."

"His whole body started jerking and then he got stiff and his eyes rolled around. Then he died."

"Did you try to revive him?"

"What, like that CPR stuff? Why would I have done that?" He chuckled. "I took him chumming for sharks."

"You took him chumming?" The catch in her voice was obvious. Piper looked at Gwen, then at Wyatt. They were watching one another's reactions closely.

"What the sharks didn't eat I tied to a block and sank out by the wreck where we fish for permit."

Piper watched Wyatt for several moments. She could tell he was fighting to maintain his composure.

"Really?" Mary Beth cleared her throat. "Have you told anyone this?"

"Just you."

"You didn't tell Wyatt?"

Wyatt's head jerked up.

"No, not even him."

"So, you sank the Jones boy by the wreck."

Robbie's laugh boomed out of the cassette player. "No. I'm just kidding you. I buried him. You don't think I'd want his sorry ass haunting my favorite fishing place do you?"

"Where did you bury him?"

"You really want to know?" He paused and Piper wondered if Mary Beth had nodded. "Spend the night with me. We'll have sex tonight and in the morning I'll take you to where the kid ended up."

A rustling made understanding the next thing Mary Beth said impossible. There were other voices muffled, then silence.

Piper jumped when Robbie spoke again. "What do you say, beautiful?"

"Stop, Robbie. You can't keep trying to get me into bed. I'm your aunt, for crying out loud. And not just by marriage, but by blood."

"Don't use that better-than-you tone with me, Mary Beth. Don't fuck with me."

The cassette clicked off. Piper could imagine Robbie speaking through clenched teeth as his last words echoed through the room. *Don't fuck with me.* Gwen's grip on her hand had become borderline painful.

†

Gwen watched from outside the ship's store as an older gentleman wearing shorts and a Guy Harvey T-shirt walked in her direction. He had a thick head of stark white hair, and fit, toned legs. He matched the description Captain Gary had given her of Dale Townsend perfectly.

So, he had come to see her as he'd said he would. *What now?* she wondered. Does she just blindly accept that he's one of the good guys? Does she hand him the letters and tape and see what he thinks they should do?

"Hi," she said. "Thanks so much for coming."

He extended his hand and she took it. "Gary and I go way back. He told me you've been wondering about that Roy Crews fellow."

"Yes, sir," she stared into his light blue eyes and felt almost mesmerized. She couldn't help wondering if those baby blues got a lot of the women of Everglades talking to him during the investigation.

"I remember him. Some people thought after he left that he was a cop but he wasn't. He was a reporter or something."

"I believe he was a private investigator," Gwen said. She didn't want to tell all too quickly, before she had a chance to decide if she trusted Dale Townsend or not.

"Crews and your mom were up to something. That much I know. And by *up to something* I don't mean having an affair or anything like that."

Gwen nodded.

"Your father was one of those guys who shook our hands and quietly went with us when it all went down. He was a gentleman."

"Yes, he was." She smiled. He was that and so much more.

"I couldn't believe when he died." Dale paused, thinking before continuing. "He was a good man down to the last minute."

Gwen narrowed her eyes as she tried to figure out what Townsend was getting at.

"You knew when he died?"

"We all did – all of us in the local law enforcement community," he said. "A lot of us didn't really think most of the regular guys deserved prison time. Some of us kind of empathized with them, you know?"

"Not enough to not bust them to begin with," Gwen said.

"No. Not that much. We were doing our jobs, that's all. Didn't mean we didn't respect some of the guys for trying to make better lives for their families. They just went about it wrong."

"You said you remember when my dad died?"

"Yeah, a couple of us agents followed that story." He shook his head. "To die like that trying to stick up for another prisoner is just wrong."

"I never heard the details of what happened. Just that he died in a prison fight." Gwen's stomach started to feel a little queasy with the memory. "He was helping someone?"

"Yeah, this skinny little black guy was being beaten regularly for being a fa – for being gay. Your dad tried to protect him one night and died for his troubles."

"Wow," Gwen whispered.

"Have you found out something about your mom and Crews?" Townsend asked.

Wyatt was of the opinion that they shouldn't share with anyone until they found their mom's remains. They were both afraid of the information they'd found either being screwed up or covered up and didn't want to take that chance. "Sort of."

"Do you want me to look at what you have?"

Those blue eyes almost tricked her into nodding in the affirmative. How could she tell him she wasn't ready to trust him yet?

He nodded his head in understanding. "Take your time. I'd like to help you, but only when you're ready."

"Thank you." She really wanted to trust him. She hated not telling him something...just in case. "If you don't hear from me again in a couple of days, would you look very closely at my cousin, Robbie Hanes?"

"Yes. And maybe when I see you in a few days, you'll tell me what this is about?"

"That's the plan."

"I interviewed both Robbie and your brother back in nineteen eighty three. To be honest, I didn't expect either one of them to stay out of prison, or alive for that matter."

She couldn't argue that point too much. This time she extended her hand. "Thanks again for coming to see me."

"It's no problem. Please promise me you'll be careful and will call me if you need anything."

An osprey called from the distance and she felt a tingling in her stomach in response. "I promise." She knew then that she could trust him. "I have a wood shop, you know, if you don't hear from me in a few days."

"I understand."

Gwen watched as Dale Townsend walked away. She wouldn't tell Wyatt how much she had told Townsend. He would be pissed at her for sure, but she felt comfortable with what she'd said to the man. She had put a copy of the video of Bronson on *Ruffled Feathers* with the cassette and letters in the wood shop. Just in case.

Wyatt didn't need to know everything she said to everyone, right? Besides, she wasn't sure how clearly he was thinking lately. Gwen was concerned that Wyatt hadn't properly grieved for Tracy yet. She was worried that he'd crash and burn and she wouldn't be able to help him.

†

Gwen took a deep breath as Wyatt beached his boat at Spider Island. "Why here?" she asked. "Of all the obscure islands, why this one?"

"I swear Robbie used to come here a lot as a kid. It just dawned on me when we were reading those letters that he don't come anywhere near here anymore. Gotta be a reason."

"Isn't this the island you guys talked about Robbie not being able to find that night we had dinner at your house, Wyatt?" PJ asked.

"That's right. You remembered that?" he asked.

"The name was memorable. Just hearing the word spider makes me cringe." She looked around.

"There ain't no more spiders here than any other island," Wyatt promised her. "It's just a name."

Gwen helped PJ down off the boat. "You can wait here, if you'd like," she offered.

"No, I'm going with you." She knocked her shoulder against Gwen's. "Now that you know all my secrets, you're stuck with me."

Gwen clasped her hand, and then released it.

Wyatt handed Gwen a spade and hand saw. "Just in case," he said when she gave him a questioning look. "You never know."

She nodded, and then led PJ under a buttonwood branch and around a clump of mangrove. When they reached a clearing, they stood up straight and Wyatt joined them. "I wonder how much of this is newer growth?"

"No telling." Wyatt studied the mangroves.

"Why is that?" PJ asked.

"Too many variables," Gwen answered. "Growth out here can be pretty erratic."

Gwen turned in small circles in the clearing. An osprey called out in the distance, and then its mate returned the call within seconds, from the other direction. Gwen walked to the edge of the mangroves and squatted down, looking deep inside.

"What'cha thinking?" Wyatt asked.

"I'm thinking about midway into that would be about the right depth to the older mangrove."

Wyatt nodded. "Yeah, little sister, I believe you're right. You want to lead the way or you want me to?"

"I will."

"Take the saw. This is important. Cut the damned prop roots if you have to. We gotta get all the way in there."

Gwen took the saw from him. "I know." She turned to PJ. "Coming in or staying here?"

"I – ah – hell, I don't know." PJ glanced all around, looking for what, Gwen wasn't sure.

"There's nothing on this island to worry about." She smiled. "Just wait right out here. This shouldn't take too long."

"Nothing to worry about but the twelve-foot pythons," Wyatt kidded.

PJ took in a sharp, deep breath.

"Don't listen to him. Even if there was one on this island it'd stay hidden and wouldn't bother you." Gwen slapped Wyatt's stomach. "Stop teasing her."

He held up his hands in mock surrender. "Come on, let's get. I don't want to still be out here when it starts to get dark."

Gwen caught a sadness in Wyatt's eyes. "You okay?" she asked him in a whisper.

"Of course I am." He pushed passed her. "I think I'll lead the way after all." He pulled a section of prop roots apart and squeezed between them. Gwen followed.

Without warning, Wyatt turned abruptly and started heading to the left.

"What do you think?" Gwen asked him.

"Not sure. This direction seems a little wider, like someone or something had a path through here at one time."

Gwen turned her body to squeeze past a root when something caught her attention. "Hey, Wyatt, wait."

"What's up?" He turned the best he could.

She studied the whitish item, following with her eyes the curve of what she finally realized was a jawbone. "Oh, Wyatt," she said through tears. There was not a doubt in her mind that they had found their mother.

He was beside her in no time. "Gwen," he whispered. "Look there. It's a second skull."

Gwen heard a slight squeal from the direction they'd come.

"Python scared your girl?" Wyatt asked.

"Let's go back. Bring both skulls and we can send the authorities in for the rest of the remains."

"What's left of them," Wyatt said as he looked around. "I'm guessing some of it's been scavenged."

Gwen felt bile burn her throat. She reached down and picked up one of the skulls. Something rattled inside and she had to fight not to vomit. "Can you reach the other?"

"Yeah," Wyatt answered, his voice tight.

They were just a few feet from the opening when Gwen stopped short and Wyatt almost ran into her. "What the hell, Gwen?"

"I'll take those," Robbie said. He pointed a gun at PJ's head. "Come on out nice and slow and maybe I won't kill her."

They stepped into the clearing. PJ was pale and looked like she might pass out.

"Set them down, one at a time, and roll them to me."

"Dude, I'm not rolling my mom's fucking head to you," Wyatt shouted.

"Hell yeah, you are. Now!" He pressed the gun harder against PJ's temple. "You first, Gwen. Do it, now."

Gwen gingerly set the skull down on the ground. She briefly shut her eyes and thought, *I'm sorry*, then rolled it toward Robbie. She looked again at PJ and regretted getting her involved in this mess.

"Now you, Wyatt."

Wyatt followed the instruction, as well. "What's your plan, Robbie?"

Robbie looked around frantically.

"You don't have one, do you?" Wyatt shook his head as he spoke. "You stupid fuck, you didn't have one then either, did you, when you killed Mom and Roy Crews?"

"I didn't need one back then. They came right to me. Who was stupid then, huh?"

Wyatt looked at the second skull more closely. "Let me guess. The bullet rattling around in this eye socket's going to match one of your guns, huh?"

"You couldn't have my mom so you killed her?" Gwen asked. "You're an even bigger loser than I always thought."

"Shut up. Shut the fuck up!" Robbie yelled as he shifted the focus of his gun from PJ's head to Gwen.

"Gwen," Wyatt said, glaring at his sister. "Let's calm down and not make matters worse, okay?"

Gwen glared back. It was okay for Wyatt to provoke Robbie but she couldn't? Then she heard the low rumble of an engine. The way sound bounced around in the backwater she knew it could be coming from – and going to – anywhere.

"Okay, okay. All of you. Put your hands on your heads and get down on your knees," Robbie commanded.

"All right, buddy, what's your plan?" Wyatt asked as he knelt down, his voice catching a little, even though it was obvious with his tone that he was trying to keep it light.

"I can't let you off this island. Not none of you." He shoved PJ in the direction where Gwen and Wyatt were kneeling. "Get down there with them," he ordered her.

"Yes, you can, Robbie, you can let us go. Take all the evidence with you and just leave. We won't say a word about any of this," Wyatt said.

Robbie shook his head. "I trust you, Wyatt, but not those bitches. They will say something, I know it."

"No," PJ pleaded. "We won't. Right, Gwen?"

"Shut up!" Robbie yelled.

"Come on, buddy, listen to me. I know you didn't think you had a choice all those years ago, but you do now." Wyatt turned to look at Robbie. "You do."

Gwen cut her eyes toward Wyatt, trying to discern if he had a plan or was just trying to buy them a little time.

They all jumped when an osprey nearby complained in a screechy voice. Gwen closed her eyes and concentrated. The osprey was pissed at something or someone getting too close to its nest. There was a rough nest on the mile marker to the east of the island, a first year, first nest for that pair. Did she hear the water lapping off the side of something solid?

Keep him talking. "Robbie, can you tell us more about what happened that day? What have you got to lose by telling us all about it?" When he stepped closer to her back but didn't speak, she continued. "Come on, cuz."

"Don't cuz me. You have never treated me like family. Even when you lived in my family's house, ate my family's food, you didn't ever act like my cuz."

"I was seven," she managed to say through her growing rage. She stopped there, deciding not to add, *and you'd just murdered my mother.*

He took the last three steps up to her and pressed the gun against the back of her head. "You look so fucking much like her that I can't wait to be able to execute her all over again."

"I told the FBI guy everything, Robbie."

"You don't know no FBI guy," Robbie said.

"Townsend is his name. Blue eyes so intense that you'd swear he's looking into your very soul?" Gwen turned and saw recognition on Robbie's face. "If I don't call Townsend tonight he's coming for you."

"I'll be long gone."

"Will you?" She hoped to shake his confidence some.

The screaming of the osprey came closer. Then another osprey answered it.

"Robbie," Wyatt whispered. "Robbie, come here for a minute, would you?"

Robbie hesitated, then after pausing beside PJ and muttering, "What a waste", he stood behind Wyatt.

"I've been good to you all these years, right?" Wyatt asked him.

"Yeah, you have."

"Then please do me a big favor, huh?"

"What?" Robbie asked.

"Kill me first."

"Wyatt," Gwen cried out.

"Seriously, Robbie. You owe me that much. I just had to watch my girlfriend die because of drugs you gave her, don't make me see you kill my sister, too."

Gwen bent forward and heaved. Robbie spun around toward her.

"Robbie," Wyatt said.

Robbie turned back to Wyatt.

"Shut up," Robbie hissed. "Your bitch girlfriend was just dragging you down. Dude, I did you a favor by switching up the pills and ensuring she croaked. You should be thanking me."

Wyatt's mouth opened but no words came out. He looked at Gwen. It occurred to Gwen that Robbie did think he did Wyatt a favor. That sent a shiver down her spine.

The ospreys' calls were getting closer and more agitated. Gwen's body vibrated with energy. Instinctively, she knew that this was the moment her entire life of reading animals was leading up to. She was sure that her sensitivity had been increasing so she would be ready for this moment. She closed her eyes briefly and had a vision. It was as if the birds were showing her what they would do so she could react. She willed Wyatt to pay attention, to for once acknowledge his gift, even if it wasn't as pronounced as hers.

"Mom and Dad will make this right," Gwen said. "Wyatt, you just have to trust in them." She flicked her gaze upward and hoped like hell that Wyatt understood.

Wyatt cocked his head but held Gwen's gaze.

There was a blur of brown and white, accompanied by harrowing screams from the pair of ospreys diving at Robbie. Robbie teetered backward but caught his balance before falling. As Robbie scrambled to keep from falling, Gwen and Wyatt both rushed him. They each had him by an arm, and Wyatt managed to wrestle the gun from him.

An explosive gun shot rang in Gwen's ears. Then another shot. She whirled around to see that Wyatt was on his stomach on the ground. PJ was still kneeling, rocking back and forth with her hands covering her ears.

Robbie was on his back, blood gushing from his chest and abdomen, his gun on the ground between him and Wyatt.

Gwen reeled around at the sound of a sob to her left. Derek stood there, wearing nothing but shorts and his old,

Anywhere, Everywhere

white crabbing boots, holding a shot gun and staring at his dying son.

"I should have rid the world of him a long time ago," he said as he reloaded the shot gun.

Gwen couldn't do anything but stay frozen, staring at the fine, gray hair covering the sagging, tanned skin of her uncle's torso. She wondered if he'd lost some weight.

Wyatt got to his feet.

PJ ran to Gwen, and Gwen pulled her close, but kept her uncle in view. His face seemed to register a moment of clarity, but then it passed and he looked confused.

Derek started shaking. When he pressed the barrel of the shot gun against the beard stubbled flesh under his chin, Gwen pressed PJ's face into her to block PJ's view. Gwen closed her eyes tight, not opening them until the next gunshot finished echoing through the mangrove roots, causing the entire island to heave with grief.

Gwen could feel Wyatt wrapping his arms around her and PJ. His body shook with sobs. She held him tighter and hoped that now he would finally grieve for Tracy.

The ospreys exchanged calls again, this time much calmer.

"Thank you," Gwen whispered.

They stayed huddled together until they heard the rumbling of multiple boat engines. Wyatt made his way to the edge of the island and Gwen heard him telling someone to get the closest wildlife officer.

Chapter Fifteen

Piper sprawled beside Gwen on the soft sand of Panther Key's beach. Her arms were tired but she felt exhilarated to have made the paddle all the way out to Panther. She was thankful that they'd be going back in with Wyatt and wouldn't need to paddle back.

Things were finally settling down. Bronson and his newly hired goons were in jail awaiting their trials. Piper hadn't heard yet if Virginia got to prosecute Bronson first or if Florida did. She didn't care, as long as he spent the rest of his days in prison.

She turned to look at Gwen. Her arms were up above her head and her body looked so inviting that Piper could hardly stand not making love to her right then and there. But now wasn't the time. Wyatt would be there shortly.

"You'll have to tell your friend Weed thanks for offering to help." She nudged Gwen's leg with her own. "Bummer I didn't get that swamp buggy ride."

Gwen nudged her back. "There's plenty of time for that. Right?"

Piper grabbed Gwen's hand and gave her a quick peck on the back of it. "Right. We have plenty of time." She turned to face Gwen. "Let me tell your story, Gwen," she said as she ran her fingertips along the tanned flesh of Gwen's thigh.

"No. I'm sorry, but I want it to be all finished."

"Don't you want the world to finally know the truth? People have told your family's story their own way for so long... don't you want the chance to tell it properly?" She hoped that Gwen trusted her to do the right thing with the story, and to give it justice in her telling of it.

Gwen reached beside her and stroked a charred piece of the paneling from the boat. It was the carving of an osprey. A fisherman had brought it to her as they were launching their kayaks. During the week, several people had delivered to her pieces of the woodwork they had found floating around. Piper was touched by how the entire community had come together in their support for Gwen and Wyatt, due to them losing *Ruffled Feathers* forever. It seemed most people just assumed, at some point, that they would regain ownership of the boat that everyone still considered part of the Martin family.

And then there was the collection that had been taken up to help pay for Tracy's cremation when her family refused to have anything to do with her in death. Piper had almost lost it when Captain Gary and Peter brought the collection to the ship's store one evening. Tears had run unchecked down both Gwen and Wyatt's faces. At that moment, Piper understood fully what the real meaning of community was.

"Okay," Gwen said.

It took a moment for Piper to realize what Gwen was saying. "Yeah?"

"But I get the final say before anything is submitted anywhere."

"Deal," Piper said as she held out her hand. Gwen clasped it, and then pulled her toward her for a hug. "You'll definitely have to help me with what is what around here. I get so confused about what's part of the Ten Thousand Islands and what's the Everglades."

"I can help you with that."

"It was hard enough for me to wrap my brain around Everglades and Everglades City meaning the same place, then there is that whole business about what is Everglades, what is Everglades National Park, and then the everglades with a lower case e."

Gwen laughed. "It's not that hard."

"Maybe not for you locals," Piper responded.

"Hey, I know of a good story for you to write. You remember that manatee I helped tow in a while back?" Gwen asked.

"The one I secretly watched you rescue?"

Gwen laughed. "Yes, that one. Duane said they're about to release her back. He's going to give me a heads-up when they do. You should come and take her picture and tell her story."

"That sounds great. I'd love to tell her story, but I'm still telling yours, too."

Gwen just nodded.

They both looked toward the water at the sound of a boat. "It's Wyatt," Piper said.

Anywhere, Everywhere

He killed the engine and held up the urn. "Y'all ready?" he asked.

Gwen approached the boat. "Don't you want to do that on your own?"

"Nope, I want my family with me." He waved to Piper. "Come on, PJ. You're part of this ragtag family now."

Piper couldn't believe how wonderful those words sounded to her.

They fit the kayaks to one side of Wyatt's boat and climbed onto the other side. "Where we headed?" Gwen asked.

"Everywhere. When Tracy was clean all she wanted to do was to go anywhere and everywhere. So, as we scoot around the backwaters, feel free to grab a handful of her ashes and send her out there." Wyatt backed the boat away from the beach.

"To anywhere and everywhere," Gwen repeated.

"To anywhere and everywhere," Wyatt and Piper said together.

About the Author

Renee MacKenzie

As a Navy brat, Renee lived on three continents before her family settled in Virginia. She currently resides in southwest Florida with her partner, Pam, and their poodle, Sabrina. Renee works and plays in the swamp, where she enjoys wildlife photography, kayaking, and hiking. Even though Renee has been paid to do all sorts of jobs, ranging from dental assistant to bartender, data entry clerk to maintenance worker, and field sampler to pet-sitter, she insists she's only had one job—writer—and all the rest has just been research.

Other Books from Affinity eBook Press

Venus Rising by Ali Spooner Levi Johnson arrives at Venus Rising, an exclusive lesbian only tropical resort in the Virgin Islands and finds more than she expected—a sizzling hot love triangle. Torn between her attraction to both women struggles to choose the right woman to share her life.

The Devil's Tree by Ali Spooner Torn between her love for the pack and her need to find what's missing in her life Devin Benoit travels to New Orleans. Will the previous happenings at the Devil's Tree help or hinder Devin in the fight of her life, and the life of Tia, the woman who now owns her heart?

The Case of the Beggars' Coppice by Erica Lawson Edda Case is a woman in crisis who discovers that things are not as they seem. Is it truly a message for her from beyond the grave or is something more sinister taking place? Can Edda solve the mystery of *The Beggars' Coppice*?

Locked Inside by Annette Mori How much does the power of love matter to someone who must overcome obstacles far greater than most people face in a lifetime.

Line of Sight by Ali Spooner Sasha and her lover Kara are back. Continue the thrilling adventures of this couple from the Sasha Thibodaux series.

Requiem for Vukovar by Angela Koenig Requiem for Vukovar continues the Refraction series and the exploits of Jeri O'Donnell and her partner, Kelly Corcoran. In an epic siege largely ignored by the wider world, Kelly, who was prepared to give up comforts and certainties when she became part of Jeri's nomadic life, encounters more than physical danger. Her ability to maintain her core integrity is assaulted by the inevitable ugliness of war. For Jeri, the true battle is confronting her attraction to violence as she struggles against losing herself in the exhilaration of combat.

Against All Odds by JM Dragon From award winning and bestselling author JM Dragon, with significant updates by, Erin O'Reilly comes an original tale of romance where everything seems to be stacked against two women whose destinies bring them together. Life however takes a twisted path setting both Steph and Louise in directions they never thought possible. Will love win out against all odds or will love be forever lost?

The Settlement by Ali Spooner The outpouring of love and friendship toward Cadin helps her on her path to healing and learning to trust her heart to love once again. Join bestselling author Ali Spooner on this sensational journey that ends with a heartwarming romance.

Once Upon a Time by Alane Hotchkin Raven only wanted to escape the blows that life had dealt her. She longed to be on the open sea and free. When she came upon a beautiful young girl sitting alone in the middle of a meadow, little did she know that her destiny would be changed forever. Will they become the pawns of the ancient vision or will both paths lead to the same port of destiny? Find out it in this exciting high seas adventure that will capture your imagination.

Asset Management by Annette Mori Follow the twists and turns to the explosive conclusion. Not everything is black and white. There are many shades of gray and sometimes it's difficult to decipher who is good and who is evil. No one is all virtue or all malevolence, but sometimes love helps us rise above.

Do Dreams Come True? by JM Dragon How do two people who really shouldn't get on end up in a relationship? Find out in this deliciously ordinary romance.

Return to Me by Erin O'Reilly Will Salvation bring just that to Ellie, allowing her to find peace and happiness again, or will it have her questioning all that she believes in? A wonderful romance cloaked within an intriguing mystery.

Arc Over Time by Jen Silver This wonderful romantic continuation with the characters from *Starting Over* ties up loose ends. But the question is—does everyone have a happy ending? A must read.

The Presence by Charlene Neal Can Rebecca and Kayleigh overcome ghosts from the past and their own insecurities, or will a presence from the past tear them apart?

A Walk Away by Lacey Schmidt Sometimes chance brings you to the right person to help you resolve some of your baggage, and you learn to like yourself a little more. Kat and Rand are smart enough to recognize this chance in each other, but they also find that there is a catch to every opportunity—walking toward something is always walking away from something else.

Possessing Morgan by Erica Lawson The investigation has barely begun when Andrea becomes the target of a nearly fatal hit-and-run. But was it really aimed at her? Can she and Morgan find the common ground they need to solve the case and stop the attacks, or are the gaps just too wide to bridge?

Twenty-three Miles by Renee MacKenzie This is a story about community, and how it comes together in dangerous and devastating times. When you don't know who to trust, you better have friends who will rally around you. Will Talia and Shay find the answers they need to the mystery of the murders on the parkway, or will justice be elusive? Will they survive their quest for the truth?

Reece's Star by TJ Vertigo   Under Faith's guiding, loving hand, will Reece successfully traverse the rocky road of emotion and embrace the positive changes in her life? Or will she panic and be unable to control that Animal part of herself? Will she take that next step to declare herself fully capable of love and devotion? This third installment in the popular series that began with *Private Dancer* continues the passionate and often hilarious romance of Reece and Faith as they both grow in love and in trust.

Confined Spaces by Renee MacKenzie   Corporate politics, complicated romance, and long distances conspire to keep Andie and Kara all boxed in. Can love triumph despite the Confined Spaces?

Cowgirl Up by Ali Spooner   Ride along with the MC2, for boot scootin', butt kickin', dirt eatin', rodeo adventures, with a love story thrown into the mix.

If I Were a Boy by Erin O'Reilly   Will Katie and Helen be able to make a life together work or succumb to doubts and the pressures of family? This story will fill you with the thrill of passion and the tenderness of love.

The Chronicles of Ratha: Book 2 A Lion Among the Lambs by Erica Lawson   Can Jordana believe in herself like her Noorthi sisters do? Only then can she fulfill her destiny as The Chosen One. Follow the colorful cast of characters in this action-packed adventure sequel as they traverse the galaxy. Of course, nothing ever goes smoothly when Jordana is involved.

Terminal Event by Ali Spooner Will the killer be caught or continue to evade authorities? Can Tally and Blair's budding romance survive the possibility? Read this intense murder mystery romance and find out.

Love Forever, Live Forever by Annette Mori Fate intervenes and puts Nicky directly back into the path of her first love, Sara, and the corresponding events send her into a tailspin. Now she must decide—who will be the person she ends up living with and loving forever?

The One by JM Dragon *2015 GCLS Winner for Romance, Intrigue, and Adventure. The One* is a romance with everything, love, intrigue, misunderstandings with a happy conclusion—the only question—who gets the girl?

Reflected Passion by Erica Lawson Through a mirror, Françoise embraces life anew, while for Dale it is a powerful awakening, forcing her to discover not only her sensual nature, but the inner strength she possesses.

Flight by Renee Mackenzie Some lives will be lost and others changed forever when the sisters' lives intersect. Will they be consumed by the wreckage, or will they be able to pick themselves up and take flight?

Affinity
eBook Press
NZ

E-Books, Print, Free e-books

Visit our website for more publications available online.

www.affinityebooks.com

Published by Affinity E-Book Press NZ LTD
Canterbury, New Zealand

Registered Company 2517228

Made in the USA
Lexington, KY
19 May 2017